Dear Reader,

Home, family, comm[unity]... values we cherish mo[st]... ground us, comfort us... [c]ertainly provide the perfect insp[iration] around which to build a romance collection that will touch the heart.

And so we are thrilled to have the opportunity to introduce you to the Harlequin Heartwarming collection. Each of these special stories is a wholesome, heartfelt romance imbued with the traditional values so important to you. They are books you can share proudly with friends and family. And the authors featured in this collection are some of the most talented storytellers writing today, including favorites such as Brenda Novak, Janice Kay Johnson, Jillian Hart and Patricia Davids. We've selected these stories especially for you based on their overriding qualities of emotion and tenderness, and they center around your favorite themes—children, weddings, second chances, the reunion of families, the quest to find a true home and, of course, sweet romance.

So curl up in your favorite chair, relax and prepare for a heartwarming reading experience!

Sincerely,

The Editors

Jillian Hart grew up on her family's homestead, where she helped raise cattle, rode horses and scribbled stories in her spare time. After earning her English degree from Whitman College, she worked in travel and advertising before selling her first novel. When Jillian isn't working on her next story, she can be found puttering in her rose garden, curled up with a good book or spending quiet evenings at home with her family.

HARLEQUIN HEARTWARMING

Jillian Hart

Sweet Home Montana

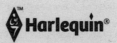

TORONTO NEW YORK LONDON
AMSTERDAM PARIS SYDNEY HAMBURG
STOCKHOLM ATHENS TOKYO MILAN MADRID
PRAGUE WARSAW BUDAPEST AUCKLAND

Recycling programs
for this product may
not exist in your area.

ISBN-13: 978-0-373-36470-1

SWEET HOME MONTANA

Copyright © 2011 by Jill Strickler

Originally published as A McKASLIN HOMECOMING
Copyright © 2007 by Jill Strickler

This edition published by arrangement with Harlequin Books S.A.

For questions and comments about the quality of this book please contact us at Customer_eCare@Harlequin.ca

® and TM are trademarks of the publisher. Trademarks indicated with ® are registered in the United States Patent and Trademark Office, the Canadian Trade Marks Office and in other countries.

www.Harlequin.com

Printed in U.S.A.

Sweet Home Montana

To Patience Smith, with my deepest thanks

Chapter One

Lauren McKaslin climbed out of her little compact sedan and into the heat of the central Montana afternoon. She looked around at the sprawling two-story house on the rise above her—her grandmother's house.

Nothing about it seemed familiar. She'd hoped to remember some part of her early childhood, jog some memory of visiting her grandmother here, but she had no memory at all. As always, the past remained as void as a black hole hovering in space, its gravity so powerful that no light or substance could escape.

She studied the surrounding countryside and tried to breathe in some of the peaceful calm, but it was impossible. She'd come to meet the grandmother she couldn't remember. The one her mother had told her had passed away.

Well, wasn't this the ultimate moment of truth? She'd driven a long way and she'd worried every mile of her trip from Southern California. Her heart beat a panicky staccato against her ribs and her hands were cold despite the ninety-six-degree shade. Since she'd started college, she'd been alone. Her mother didn't approve.

Please, let this turn out like I hope. I really want a family. It wasn't only her grandmother she'd come to meet. That was a scary thought, too.

The gravel crunched beneath the soles of her worn-out rubber flip-flops. Her throat was dry as she closed her car door. It sounded like a slam in the far-reaching stillness. The only other sound was the whisper of the hot breeze in the maples overhead.

It's going to be okay, Lauren. Remember how nice Gran was on the phone? But that didn't stop the anxiety washing through her. Shyness rolled over her in a wave. But something worse, something as heavy as lead, was sitting in the middle of her stomach. Fear. Maybe it was because of her mother's response when, as a teenager, she'd wanted to contact her long-lost family. *She won't want you any more than she wanted me. Go ahead. You'll see. As for the rest of 'em, they didn't want you then, they won't want you now.*

Her life had been so bleak at the time, those words had seemed reasonable. And for the last few years she'd been afraid to find out. What if she learned her mother was right?

Don't think about that, Lauren. Her mom had rarely been right about anything. She was probably wrong about this, too. Still, the doubt had taken hold and, like a vicious dog, had sunk in its teeth and would not let go. She felt very small standing in the shade of the enormous, upscale house. Even while she smoothed at the wrinkles in her walking shorts, she imagined she was very rumpled.

"Hello there."

She startled at the rumble of a man's voice—vibrant and resonant and deep. Then she saw him. He was nothing more than a part of the shadows in the shade of the porch. The shadow became a tall, wide-shouldered man. As he ambled toward her with an easygoing stride, he came into the touch of the dappled sunlight and she could see him clearly. He had a rugged, granite look to him. Dark brown hair tumbled over a high forehead. A confident sloping nose, a hard line of mouth, dark eyes and a chiseled jaw all complemented his square, handsome face. His big hands gripped the polished porch rail as he focused on her.

Shyness rolled over her in a bigger wave. Who was he? Before she could get up the courage to ask, he walked down the steps in her direction.

"Are you looking for Mary?"

She nodded, realizing that with every step he took, he became bigger. Not that he was scary looking, it was just that she didn't trust men that much. Also, as far as she could tell, Lauren and the man were absolutely alone, aside from the half-dozen horses in the field beyond the impressive house and the acres of grass and white rail fencing and fruit trees. She liked to keep her distance from strange men.

But then he smiled and that simple change softened his strong features. He was near enough that she could see the warmth of his eyes, which had initially seemed so dark. There was friendliness in those depths.

Nothing to be worried about. She'd grown up in the inner city and old habits died hard. "Y-yes, I'm looking for Mary. She's expecting me."

"All I know is that she gave me a call about thirty minutes back, said she was running late and asked me to be here to meet her houseguest. I suppose that would be you?" He arched one brow and this, along with his grin, made him look like a stalwart, salt-of-the-earth kind of guy.

Not that she was one to believe in that kind of thing, but he was clearly a trusted neighbor of her grandmother's. Her uncertainty ebbed a bit. "She's running late? I can just sit here and wait for her."

"In this heat? Come in and I'll get you settled. She said she wouldn't be long." He kept coming—all six-plus feet of him—moving like a muscled tiger, sleek and confident and powerful. "I'm Caleb Stone. I live next door."

"Next door? I only see horses next door."

His grin widened, revealing a double set of dimples. "That means down the road. You're a long way from home. I noticed your California license plate."

"Uh, I'm just here for a quick visit. This part of the country is beautiful. Secluded, but beautiful."

And so was she, Caleb Stone thought. When Mary had called him up, interrupting him in the middle of fixing his after-work supper, he'd wanted to know the who and what of her request. She'd been tight-lipped about it. He'd been curious about her keeping quiet, but now he understood. The family resemblance was pretty strong and that meant that this woman could only be the lost granddaughter come home.

"You're Lauren, aren't you?" He said it in a friendly way because she seemed like a worrier. She glanced uncertainly around her with wide eyes; her hands, holding on to her keys and backpack strap, were white-knuckled. She stood perfectly still next to her decades-old sedan, looking wholesome in a simple summer shirt and modest shorts.

"How do you know who I am?"

"There's a strong family resemblance. I didn't know that Mary had kept in touch with you."

"She hadn't. This was all sort of a last-minute thing."

Interesting. "It's a long way to come at the drop of a hat."

"Yes. Do you know how long Mary plans to be?"

He came closer until he could see the light scatter of freckles across the bridge of her nose and the uncertainty on her heart-shaped face. "She said I ought to get you settled."

"I don't feel right going into her house without her. If you don't mind, I'll just wait in the shade for her. And you can go home. It's dinnertime. You must have plans."

"I've got lots of time." He wondered about her, this granddaughter and sister no one had talked about in, what, twenty years? It was as if she'd died, right along with the mother who'd taken her and fled all those years ago, destroying the family. Yep, call him curious.

"I've got no place else to be, so I'd be happy to get your things. Want to unlock your trunk for me? I'll get your bags."

"Oh, I don't mind doing it. Really." She whirled around and with a snap of her flip-flops was heading toward the back of her little old sedan.

He'd been reading people for a lot of years—it came with being a cop—and there was something about her, something essentially lonely about her. He couldn't pinpoint it. Maybe it was the hesitant way she'd greeted him or her reserved manner. As he followed her to the back of her car, where she was unlocking the trunk with the twist of a key, he held back his questions. He had a lot of them. Mary had buried her husband more than two years ago and she'd never come back from the blow of his sudden loss. He wondered why Lauren hadn't stayed in contact with the family. What had she been doing all this time? And, the toughest question of all— was she anything like that mother of hers? He didn't think so, but sometimes people hid the most crucial information.

There were two medium-sized duffel bags

in the tidy trunk and he'd beat her to them. "Don't worry, I've got them."

"But—"

"You're in Montana now. You'll have to get used to men being men." He flashed her his most disarming grin and shut the trunk. "Hey, don't worry. Most of the time I'm perfectly harmless."

"And what about the rest of the time?"

"I'll let you figure that out."

That's when it happened. Her reserve melted away and she smiled. Just a little, but the effect was dazzling. She sure looked like goodness. That was one image he wanted to believe.

Then he saw something else beyond Lauren's shoulder—a streak of white against the amber-tipped grasses of the horse pasture. The swinging gate was wide open. Unless his eyes were playing tricks on him, Malia was up to her old tricks. That troublesome mare!

He set the bags on the walkway's top stone step. "How good are you at herding horses?"

Lauren missed a step. Had she heard him right? Had he said—"herding horses"?

"We have an escapee."

"What?" Then she turned to follow his gaze and saw the open gate and the horses racing away down the gravel driveway, tails flying.

"C'mon." He flashed her that dimpled grin in a way that made him seem like the perfect Western man. He gestured toward the detached garage set so far back she could only see the front doors.

"I don't know how much help I'll be."

"You'll do fine, city girl." He said those words warmly, but there was a hint of something else underneath.

Lauren wasn't sure she ought to step into a vehicle with a stranger, but he was already running. She watched as he disappeared around the side of the house's raised flower beds. Should she accept his request? How could she help? He might be a stranger to her, but it was clear her grandmother relied on him. Okay, so she had trust issues. It was simply an old habit—and a hard-learned lesson in her life—that you were better off keeping to yourself. Strangers were people who hadn't taken advantage of you yet. Or, in most cases when she was growing up, people who hadn't taken advantage of her mother yet.

The best defense was a solid independent streak and a look that sent people scurrying. This time she was having difficulty summoning up that look or the belief that Caleb Stone wasn't just how he seemed—an all right guy. He drove into sight in a blue medium-sized pickup with the window rolled down. Leaning out, he met her gaze. His truck ground to a halt in the gravel, kicking up a cloud of dust.

"Get in. Your grandmother's horses are getting away." His grin broadened and the big rugged man became someone else with that smile. His dark eyes crinkled pleasantly in the corners. The hard angles of his face softened. Everything about him screamed capable. Trustworthy. Honest.

"I *should* help with my grandmother's horses."

His eyes twinkled. "Exactly. It's the least you could do."

Maybe part of it was that she really wanted to see those horses. Her grandmother hadn't mentioned owning horses! She reached for the door but it was already swinging open. There Caleb was, straightening back to the wheel.

Okay, so he was a gentleman, too. She hopped onto the seat and the truck was already in motion as she reached for the seat belt. The air conditioner was blowing against the sun-warmed passenger compartment and the windows were down, the fresh dust-scented air blowing against her face.

"Glad you came along. I could use the company." He reached around to grab his Stetson from above the back window. "Besides, it's always less exasperating when you share the load with someone."

"Exasperating? That's making me regret that I came along."

"Then forget that I said *exasperating.* Pretend I said *interesting* instead."

"That's not giving me a lot of confidence."

"Don't you worry. There's no reason you shouldn't trust me. I know what I'm doing. I've been doing this since I was a little guy."

It was hard to imagine this big man as a "little guy." But before she could think about it too much, his rugged baritone stopped the direction of her thoughts.

"There they are. Look at 'em go."

As the truck curved around the bend in the road, the escaped horses came into sight. Four horses, their rich velvet colors glistening in the sunshine, their manes and tails flying in the wind, their dainty legs reaching out powerfully and their hooves churning up the ground.

Thrills shivered through her, and she leaned forward. She'd never been this close to horses before.

"Malia's the lead mare, the white Arabian," Caleb explained. "She must be real proud of herself, figuring out that new lock I installed. Took her long enough, the rascal."

"They're beautiful, all color and grace and motion." She itched for her sketch pad so she could put the image of them on the page. She tried to memorize the way the sunlight glossed their flanks of black, brown and white.

"They know they're in trouble. Look at 'em."

Lauren watched in amazement as the horses fell into a single line at the shoulder of the road, as if to make room for the truck to catch up with them. A warm breeze skittered over her face, tangling her hair, as they raced closer and closer to the horses.

"They're havin' fun." Caleb shouted to be heard over the pounding hoof beats and rush of wind through the cab. "Watch, now, how Malia stretches out. She likes to stay in the lead. She's getting a kick out of this."

Surely this couldn't be safe. She knew the driveway ended around the next turn in the road, which she could see up ahead. They were neck and neck with the last horse of the small herd, giving Lauren a closer look. Foam flecked those sleek glossy coats, but she felt their happiness as they ran free and safe, penned in between the truck and the long, endless row of fencing.

"You think this is fun?" she asked. "What happens when you hit the main road?"

"You'll see. This isn't the first time we've done this."

"Isn't this a little dangerous?"

"It's a private road." He didn't seem concerned, but she wasn't fooled. He kept a careful watch on the driveway up ahead and on the horses to make sure there was plenty of space between his truck's fender and the wide grassy shoulder the horses were running on.

When the road curved to the left, the horses kept following the fence line, wheeling right like a flock of close-knit birds. The truck swung wider, keeping up with them, bouncing over wild grasses and wildflowers. Up ahead, an intersecting fence line cut off the horse's charge. As if the horses knew just what would happen, all but the leader began to slow. Their run for freedom was over. Caleb skidded the pickup to a fast sliding stop, nosing up close to the fence, corralling the horses safely. Lauren watched in amazement as the white mare sailed over the six-foot rail.

"She's mad at me today. She's probably jealous of you." He swung out of the truck and went to the horses.

"Of me?" she called out to him.

"Sure. She's the only female in my life."

When she twisted around in her seat, she caught a view of him in the side mirror. He was reaching into the back of the truck for a handful of colored nylon ropes, all the while talking low to the horses.

The dust was settling and she could see the friendliness between the man and the horses, who seemed to know him well. If she opened the door, would it startle them? She was way out of her element here, but Caleb had said he needed help. She leaned out the open window, studying the enormous horses from the safety of her seat. They were much larger and more powerful up close. One of them snorted and stomped its front foot like a bull getting ready to charge. Definitely not safe just yet.

"Leopold, stop showin' off for the lady." Caleb shook his head, tossing a look to her. "Lauren, he's such a show-off. It's okay to come on out. I could use a little help."

"You don't look like it."

"It's always good to share the load." He snapped a rope onto the stomping horse. "You, buddy, calm down. Yes, we're all impressed with you."

Lauren opened the door, watching as the other horses sidestepped in response. They watched her with what she hoped was interest—and not dislike. She felt very small next to the animals and she was in awe. Caleb snapped a rope onto another horse's halter

and the remaining two animals looked mis-
chievously at the opening, beyond Caleb.

"No, you don't." He'd noticed, too. "Lauren,
would you mind standing behind me. These
two still have a few ideas."

She was already moving through the sun-
baked grass that tickled her ankles. "And
exactly how do you think I'm going to stop
them if they act on their ideas?"

"Well, I'm banking on the hope that they'll
believe your bluff."

"I don't bluff."

"We might be in trouble, then." He didn't
look troubled by it as he went after horse
number three.

It was hard not to like Caleb, Lauren decided. The sunlight chose that moment to find
him, highlighting his stony quiet strength.
Like some Western hero of old, he approached the last free horse with a low word,
brushed his big hand over the animal's vel-
vety nose. He made an image of rugged mas-
culinity that made even her want to believe.

"Lauren, would you mind driving the truck
back for me? I've got my hands full."

"What about Malia?"

"Don't you worry, I've got her number." He reached into the back of the truck and held out brown squares. It had to be some kind of horse treat. Amusement sparkled in his dark eyes. "Watch."

He offered a cube to each horse and, sure enough, the breathtaking white mare hung her head over the board-rail fencing, nickering for her share of the treats.

"Sorry, Malia. You've got to come to me if you want some." Caleb didn't seem too troubled. As he gave attention to the other horses, Malia sailed back over the fence and pranced up to him, expecting her treat.

Wow. Lauren held down a sigh. The wind blew against her face, tangling her hair and breezing over her like a reassuring touch. The struggle of her life seemed far away.

She was glad that she'd come all this way.

Chapter Two

"What are you doing carrying your own bags?" Caleb didn't mean to startle her, but he could see by the look on her face that he had. There she was, teetering up the walkway toward the porch steps, a heavy, battered duffel in each hand. While the bags weren't big, they were heavy. He remembered that. "Put 'em down. You're in Montana now. I can't let a woman do the heavy work while I watch."

"Isn't that a little chauvinist?"

"Maybe where you're from, but I call it doing the right thing." He crossed over

Mary's lawn. "Besides, you don't know where you're going."

"Uh, how about into the house?"

"So you think." What was a guy to do? "It's one thing to have an independent streak, it's another to let a man stand around gettin' lazy."

That made her smile and he liked this because her shyness faded away and her unique loveliness shone.

"One thing I don't approve of is a lazy man." Amusement warmed the violet of her eyes. "I suppose I should put you to work and keep you respectably useful."

"Exactly. It's for the greater good."

She lowered the bags with a thud at his feet.

"Mary has the carriage house ready for you, out back." He got a good grip on the crackled handles of the bags and heaved. "Are there rocks in here? Weights? Or really big shoes?"

"Books."

That explained it. He'd noticed the backpack. "Are you a student?"

"Yep. Classes start in three weeks."

She was a little old for a college girl, although she might be putting herself through school. That could slow a student down, working full-time and juggling classes. He should have noticed the little details. Her car was twenty years old and if he'd described it as having seen better days, he would have been kind. She was as neat as a pin, but her clothes were simple and not exactly designer. Her flip-flops were wearing thin. And then there was the backpack—typical student ware.

Curious, he led the way along the path curving around the house. "What's your major?"

"I'm finishing up a master's in business. Hey, don't look so surprised."

"You want to be a businesswoman?"

"A lot of people do. Why?"

How did he say it? "For some reason I figured, since you lived in L.A.—"

"You thought I'd be like my mom and want to be an actress." Hurt shadowed her eyes and dimmed her smile.

"Hey, I didn't mean any insult."

"I get that a lot." She shrugged one slim shoulder, as if it were no big deal.

Caleb figured it was. There was something about her, something he still couldn't put his finger on. But there was a lot to like about her.

"Oh, there are the horses." She changed the subject as they circled around the side of the house. "I hope the gate is secure."

"I roped it up good. It's gotten to be a sort of game to Malia. She's smart, I've got to give her credit for that. I'll have to order a new latch and hope it's the one she won't be able to figure out. Thanks for your help back there. If you hadn't driven the truck back, right now I'd be walking in the hot sun to fetch it. Would you like something to cool you off?"

Suddenly his voice sounded distant and tinny. What was happening? Lauren's feet froze in place at the top of the walk. Emotion spun through her, unnamed and misty, like fog rolling in with the Pacific's tides. Was it a memory of the past? Or the wish for one?

"Are you okay?" Caleb stopped, reversed and came to stand in front of her. His big shadow fell across her and it felt oddly intimate. "You're pale all of a sudden."

"I just…I think I remember this place."

It was there, just beyond her reach, an image she couldn't bring into focus. It remained fuzzy, hidden by the mist of twenty years, but it *was* there. A voice she couldn't hear, a faint scent of apples and cinnamon. Leaves rustling through the trees and a feeling she couldn't pin down that remained cloaked in fog.

The hint of memory disappeared, leaving her empty and alone. Her heart ached with loss and she didn't know why.

"It doesn't seem like a very good memory."

Caleb's voice surprised her. For a moment it was as if she were alone in the dappled sunlight. But he was there, towering so close he filled her field of vision.

"Why don't you sit down," he suggested, "right here out of the sun."

There was something in his words, something kind and unexpected. Caleb Stone took her arm, his strong hand cupping her elbow, and guided her. She sank onto the bottom step of the porch, shaded by the house and the overhead trees.

Caleb's hand moved to her shoulder. A comforting gesture. He clearly thought she was ill. "It's over a hundred in the shade. This mountain air is so dry, you dehydrate before you know it. I kept you out in the sun too long."

Her chest twisted so tight, she couldn't answer. She didn't think it was the heat and sun that was affecting her so much. It was the past and this reaction was something she hadn't expected. She hadn't come here to dredge up hurt. No, she'd come out of curiosity. She wanted to know where she'd come from. Who she was. Maybe that would help her figure out better where she was headed in life.

"You stay right here." His big fingers squeezed once, gentle and soothing, sending a rush of peace through her troubled heart. "I'll be right back."

His boots knelled against the wood steps and the wraparound porch. A screen door squeaked open somewhere at the side of the house.

The pressure in her chest increased. Was she upset by this stranger's kindness? Or from memories, unseen and without shape, remembered in her heart? And why? Why had it always remained a blank? Mom refused to talk about the past. Refused to say if there were any siblings, a father, cousins, aunts and uncles, grandparents left behind. People that might have mattered to her.

Caleb's steps approached her from behind with an easygoing cadence. She heard ice tinkling in a glass. "Here."

She stared at the tall glass of lemonade he offered. The scent was bright and sour-sweet as he lowered the glass into her hand.

"You're still not looking too well. Did you drive straight through?"

She shook her head. Took the glass. Stared at the lemony goodness. Here was the edge of that memory. She tasted the lemonade and already knew the flavorful and sweet-tart taste before it hit her tongue. Frustrated, she wished there was more to her recollection.

"You rest here. Rehydrate." Caleb rose. He remained behind her, out of her sight, but his presence was substantial all the same. "I'll take your bags out to the carriage house."

It had been a long time since anyone had helped her. "Thanks, Caleb."

"Sure thing." Then he was gone, leaving her alone with the glass of lemonade.

Maybe her lack of memory was a sign. Her mind had buried something so deep on purpose—to protect her, or because it hadn't mattered. She wanted answers, but what if she didn't like what she found out?

I could get hurt.

Uncertainty and regret swirled into a black mass in the middle of her stomach. Her hands began to tremble, sloshing the lemonade around in the tall cool glass.

What would her grandmother think of her? Would there be disappointment on her face? Would she, like her daughter, Lauren's mother, find so much to criticize?

So many worries. She took a shaky breath, trying to pull herself together. Hot wind breezed against her face like a touch, reminding her of where she was. The drum of a man's sure and leisurely gait sounded on the porch boards behind her. She could feel the vibration of his steps roll through her.

Lauren couldn't exactly say why she was so aware of Caleb Stone's presence.

He sat next to her and shaded his eyes with

one broad, sun-browned hand. He gazed down the long stretch of gravel driveway. "You feel a little nervous about all this?"

"Something like that." Although nervous didn't begin to describe it. As nice as Caleb seemed, he was a stranger to her, and she didn't feel comfortable talking about something so private. Time to change the subject. "The horses are all right?"

"I've got to get back and give them a rub down and a little water, but I had to see to you first. It can't be easy coming back after all these years."

"Coming back? I don't remember this place at all. Nothing."

"You were pretty young when you left."

"When my mother took me." There was a difference. All she could remember was crying and then choking on her own sobs, bouncing around on the vinyl backseat of her mom's 1962 Ford as they drove away forever. She'd been two. She could still hear her mom's voice, trembling with that high, nervous tone she had when everything was going wrong. *"We're meant for better things, you and me. You'll see, sweetness."*

Better things had been a long string of shabby apartments—and sometimes worse—until Lauren had struck out on her own. In a way, she'd always been alone. She didn't mind it. She'd never known anything else.

He broke into her thoughts. "I'm good friends with your brother. Spence. I know your sisters real well."

"Then you're not only a neighbor, but a family friend."

"You could say that."

But what wasn't he saying, Lauren wondered. Was he starting to piece things together and beginning to wonder about her? If she was like her mother? She took a sip of lemonade. The flavor burst across her tongue more sweet than tart and that tugged at lost memories, too.

Although she didn't say anything, Caleb kept talking. He steepled his hands. "Do you remember your brother at all? He's the oldest. You know that, right?"

The lemonade caught halfway down, sticking like a heavy ball in her throat, turning sour. No longer sweet. "My grandmother had mentioned my brother and sisters. But I don't remember them."

"You don't even remember your family?"

She couldn't swallow. It was even more impossible to talk. She stared at her flip-flops, blue to match her summer top. It felt shameful, not to remember. Like she didn't care enough to, but that wasn't right. More like she was afraid to remember anything that happened before sitting on that backseat with her mother scolding her to shut up. Lauren remembered biting down on her lip to keep the sobs inside and staring hard at her little denim sneakers with the orange laces.

She'd only allowed herself to cry in private since.

Now she felt a hot burn behind her eyes and her vision blurred. "I was hoping to find out that my mother was wrong. That they hadn't forgotten me. That they didn't want me to go in the first place."

Caleb didn't get it. He knew mostly from rumor about the mother, of course. It had been a terrible shame for the family, how the young mother of five had run away, abandoning her home and husband and older children. "Why did you wait so long?"

"It's complicated. And p-painful." She shrugged a slender shoulder—too slender of a shoulder.

He believed her. "I'm sorry. I didn't mean to bring up anything painful."

"Being here is painful. My mom wasn't exactly honest. She said that I didn't have any grandparents who were still alive. And that the family, well—" she paused. "They hadn't w-wanted us. Me. That my father signed me away."

"That wasn't the case. It's not my business and I'm only a friend, but I do know that much. Look. There's your grandmother."

A gleam at the far bend in the driveway caught her attention. A faint cloud of dust rose up behind an oncoming vehicle. Her grandmother? Lauren's heart kicked hard against her sternum. Nerves roiled up again. And the worries. What if this didn't go as well as she hoped? What if she was a disappointment to her grandmother? Or her grandmother to her?

You can do this, Lauren.

She took a steady breath, sat up straight and set the glass of lemonade down on the step, up against the newel so it would be out of the way. Sunlight reflected off the oncoming windshield. Eternity passed while she watched that vehicle in the distance take shape and form and color. A gray, perfectly shined luxury sedan rolled to a stop alongside her rattletrap car.

The hood ornament glinted like an unreachable promise and there was a woman, gray-haired and somber, staring at her over the hood. Hard to tell behind the dark designer sunglasses what her first impression of Lauren was, but her mouth was a straight, unsmiling line.

She is disappointed in me. Lauren's heart fell to the floor. Emotion wedged so tight in her throat she couldn't swallow. She tried to rise, but her knees were too weak. Had she come all this way for nothing?

Then she felt a rock-solid hand at her elbow. A man's big hand cupped her elbow and steadied her in comfort and support. She fought the urge to step away; his touch calmed her and she didn't mind leaning on him, just a little. When she turned to thank him his steady eyes were soft with kindness. *Kindness.*

"It'll be fine." He sounded so sure. As sure as his hold on her arm helping her to stand.

His words and his decency made all the difference. Her knees felt watery, but they held her weight as she stood in the dappled sunlight and felt her grandmother's scrutiny. The car door whispered open and the woman emerged. She had sleek silver hair cut in a bob that curled thickly at her jawline. Porcelain skin. A dainty chin. The lines of her face were crisp and clean and familiar. Like her mother's. Like her own.

But the elegance and grace of the woman, the power and dignity were different. Mary Whitman commanded attention. She took a regal step forward. Dressed in quality clothes, she looked casual and tasteful. She wore sleek tailored tan slacks and a coordinating cashmere cardigan and mock-turtleneck shell. Accents of gold—fine gold, no fourteen-karat stuff—glinted at her earlobes and throat, wrist and fingers. Her designer purse and shoes matched perfectly and looked pristine, unscuffed.

Lauren had never felt so small. She felt painfully aware of her wrinkled khaki shorts and her simple summer top—not exactly designer or the latest fashion. Her discount-store rubber flip-flops were nearly worn out.

Only now did it occur to her that maybe she should have stopped at a fast-food place and used the bathroom to change into nicer clothes. With a sinking feeling, she had to admit that nothing in her wardrobe would make a better impression on this woman. She'd assumed her mother had come from simple beginnings.

She smoothed the wrinkled cuff of her shorts and tasted her nervousness. "It's nice to finally meet you in person. I'm Lauren."

Okay, that was obvious. But the woman— her grandmother—wasn't saying anything. She just stood there, one hand resting on the side of her car door, not moving a muscle.

It was Caleb Stone who broke the silence. "Mary, are you all right?"

He dropped his grip on Lauren's arm and moved forward. In that moment, Lauren saw the caring. The genuine concern. He had a good heart.

"No." The older woman nearly choked on the word. She lifted her hand to her chest, pressing against her throat. "The sight of her simply knocks the breath from me. Lauren, you're the spitting image. It's just uncanny."

"Of Katherine?" Caleb asked.

Lauren didn't know who Katherine was. She was only aware of the pain beginning to fill her chest.

It's my mom, she thought, knowing there had been a terrible rift between her grandmother and mother, something horrible enough for each to ignore the other for two decades. Without a doubt it was her mom's fault.

"I—I look like L-Linda, I know." Her voice caught on her mother's name, or maybe it was the swirling emotions and fears that made her stutter. "But I'm n-nothing like her. I don't want to upset you."

"No, I'm not upset. Just surprised." Mary Whitman took off her sunglasses, exposing gentle green eyes brimming with tears. "You look something like Linda, true, but heavens, look at you. You're the very image of my sister, gone this last year. It's like she's come to life again. Goodness. Come closer, child."

I don't remember this woman, Lauren thought, taking a stumbling step forward. But she wanted to. With all of her heart. Surely there were some memories tucked away. She tried to resurrect them. Images of homemade cookies or hot chocolate—but there was only a blank. Nothing at all. No recollections of a younger-looking version of this woman before the silver hair and the gentle wrinkles.

Mary Whitman stood tall with a poise that came from a lifetime of rising above adversity. Lauren could sense it, see it in the dignity of the woman's tear-filled eyes. Tears that did not fall. Her arms stretched out, eager for a hug.

Lauren came from a childhood without a lot of affection. She couldn't remember the last time her mother had hugged her. The thought was uncomfortable, but she stumbled forward anyway and into the circle of her grandmother's embrace.

Lilacs. Mary smelled of lilacs. It was a

scent Lauren remembered. Somewhere in the vast shadows of her early childhood, she saw the glimmer of memory just out of reach, bobbing closer to the surface.

It was a start.

Chapter Three

Over her grandmother's shoulder, Lauren caught sight of Caleb's slow, silent retreat. He held her lemonade glass in one hand as he backed away. Their gazes met. For one instant, the breeze stopped blowing. Her heart stilled and the tightness in her chest faded.

"I told you." He mouthed the words, lifted a hand in farewell and headed silently out of sight, leaving behind the impression of his kindness. A kindness she appreciated.

Mary released her from the hug, but held tight to her hand, as if she were determined not to let go.

Strange, Lauren had come here feeling vulnerable, but this woman's arm was so frail, nothing but fragile bones and a silk sleeve. Lauren took a more guiding hold on her to make sure she was all right. "You look like you need to sit down."

"No, dear. Just taken back. You wouldn't remember my dear sister. Cancer took her. There isn't a day that goes by that I don't miss her sorely."

"I'm sorry." She couldn't imagine what that must be like, to miss someone so much. To love them so much.

Judging by the pain stark on her grandmother's face and how it seemed to drain her of strength, Lauren decided that she might live a lonely life, but maybe she was lucky, in a way. She would never know her grandmother's sorrow and loss and heartbreak.

Maybe that was better, to be safe from that kind of pain.

"I'm *so* glad you've come. Now, let me get a good look at you. My, how you've grown. A little underfed, but that's an easy remedy. I can't get over it. All this time." Tears silvered Mary's eyes. "Twenty-two years just flew by and it's an eternity all the same. It's been enough for the sweet little toddler you were to grow up. You don't remember me at all, do you?"

"No, but I wish I did."

"Well, here I'm going on and on and you must be tired from such a long drive. You must have come up through Utah."

"I did. It was a gorgeous drive. It's lovely here, too."

"I think so, too. It's home." Mary slipped her arm through Lauren's. "I hope you don't mind I've put you out here."

Sadness seemed to stick with the older woman and her voice was brittle sounding. Lauren didn't know what to say or how to make it better. She looked up to realize there was an in-ground pool to her left, glittering around an enormous brick patio. Ahead, there was a garden gate that led to a small cottage, hidden behind climbing roses and flowering shrubs.

It was sweet, like something out of a gardener's dream.

"This used to be my studio, and then a guest house. Your sister Katherine lived here for a long while, until she got her own place in town. Caleb stayed here when he went to college. He lives next door now, and takes care of the place for me when I'm gone. These days I spend most of my time in Arizona." Mary led the way along the cozy porch to the front door. "Speaking of Caleb, where did he get off to?"

"To see to the horses, I think."

"He's a fine man. I don't know what I would do without him. I've known him since he was a wee thing. He's a man a woman can count on."

How could she tell her grandmother that she hadn't thought that a man like that existed on this entire planet? Mary obviously held Caleb in high regard and for good reason. The image of him in his cowboy hat, calming the horses seemed implanted in Lauren's brain. There was goodness in him and a lot of dependability. Even she could see that. But a lot of men were that way—except when it really counted.

"I thought you might be more comfortable out here," Mary was saying as they ambled along the flagstone path to the little cottage.

"You'll have your privacy. I know this is going to be a lot for you to adjust to, meeting your family. There are a lot of us."

"It's already overwhelming. But nice."

Mary's beaming smile was reward enough. Lauren was deeply glad that she'd come. No matter what. A flicker of joy filled her right up. She, who'd always felt so alone, had a grandmother—a real one, a caring one. It was hard not to care right back. And didn't that mean she was completely out of her element?

Yes.

The little house had a fan-shaped window in the rounded top of the door. It was like a storybook cottage.

Another clue that she was out of her comfort zone. Inside, the cottage was as sweet as promised from the outside, with sheer white curtains swinging in the breeze from the open windows, gleaming honey-wood floors and a cabbage rose covered couch. There was a matching chair and ottoman, which looked good for reading, and scarred end tables topped with colorful pottery lamps. Lauren spotted a tiny kitchen in the corner, with an avocado-green stove and refrigerator. The place was so homey, she was afraid to believe it was real.

Just like with Mary.

"You go ahead and freshen up, dear. I know it was a long, hot and dusty drive. I had Caleb stock the little kitchen with a few necessities, so poke around if you like. When you're ready, come up to the main house. I should have supper on the table in thirty minutes."

"Yes, ma'am."

During the whole trip Lauren had wondered what she would say to her grandmother. She'd made a mental list of the questions to ask and of the things she needed to know. Now those questions flitted away like dry leaves in the wind, rolling out of sight.

She felt lost. Nothing was as she expected it to be.

Mary reached out and squeezed her hand. The contact wasn't something she was used to, but for that one microsecond, the vast canyon she always kept between her and everyone else was bridged. She was no longer painfully alone.

Then Mary let go and stepped away. The canyon around her returned and she didn't know what to say next. She wrapped her arms around her middle, but that was no comfort from the loneliness.

She was trailing her grandmother to the open door, to close it after her, when she spotted a framed picture hung on the wall. It was one among many with unfamiliar smiling faces, but this photograph called to her.

"Oh, that's you right there." Mary brushed a manicured fingertip toward the family portrait. "Do you remember?"

"Not really." She stared at herself, the little girl in the photograph, chubby with the look of a tot who was more infant than toddler, dressed in a poufy white-and-blue sailor dress and bonnet. She sat on her mother's lap. She recognized her mom, of course. Perhaps that was what had made her stop in the first place.

She studied the face of the tall, capable-looking man standing behind Mom. She didn't recognize her father's face, which was more lean than round, with a hawk-like nose and square jaw. He had a friendly look to him.

Her dad. The dad who'd never wanted to see her. She swallowed hard against the pain.

Maybe what her mother had told her about her father was not true, either. Why didn't she remember him? Or her brother and sisters? Her brother was a tall, teenage boy who closely resembled their father. There were three other girls—a slim preteen, who had wide eyes and a pretty smile even with braces, and two grade-school girls who were shockingly identical.

Twins? Lauren didn't even know there were twins in the family. Her family. People she was connected to by blood, but nothing else. They were simply strangers.

Strangers.

She studied the smiling family. The clothes were dated, fashionable twenty years ago and of modest department-store quality. The kids had the same blond hair and violet-blue eyes that she had.

An eerie feeling of recognition crawled through her, but it was nothing she could grasp. No tangible memory came to the surface through the void.

"That's your father, of course. He's remarried. Spence runs the family bookstore these days, along with Katherine. You won't be meeting her on this visit, since she's off on her honeymoon. The twins are Aubrey and Ava. Of course, they're all grown up now. Don't think, because you didn't grow up here, that you were out of my thoughts or my heart, because that wouldn't be true. You're my granddaughter, regardless of what your mother did."

How could that be said so simply, as if Linda hadn't done everything she could to upset and bribe and wheedle money out of Mary? Lauren swallowed hard against the memories that settled like a boulder in her throat. She may have been very young, but she remembered many of mom's phone calls and how she'd behaved. It all made sense now. Is that the kind of person she seemed like to Mary, someone like her mother?

She looked again at her mother's face, young and unlined, sun browned, even back then, to a shocking shade. The striking woman in the pretty blue dress that matched the light shade of her eyes and her hair in a sleek bob *resembled* her mom. But Lauren didn't know this woman. The mother she knew never would have been anything like the calm, cheerful-looking woman in the photograph.

Lauren felt even more alone, a stranger to herself.

Her grandmother broke the silence. "I'm terribly glad you're home now. I'd best go put the potatoes on. You must be hungry."

Lauren's heart stood still. She saw the older woman to the door and waited a moment to close it so she could memorize her grandmother's figure—her natural poise, straight spine, her slenderness and elegance. Mary walked through the little picket gate, where an arbor thick with red roses arched overhead, and then disappeared from view.

This was *not* what she'd been expecting. Boy, talk about being out of her comfort zone. Lauren closed the door and leaned against it. She was just tired, that's why she felt so fragile. She blinked back the rising tears in her eyes. She'd come to find the truth. She had a feeling the truth was something she wasn't going to like.

Still, it was hard not to adore her grandmother. She seemed like the nicest person. She'd come thinking, at best, she would meet this lady. And now she had to wonder if there was a chance finally to have a real family tie. Or was this welcome simply to satisfy curiosity? A meeting and then that was all. Her grandmother would see her granddaughter all grown up, and she would have answers.

Tucking away her hopes, Lauren went in search of her bags, which she found on a little cedar chest at the foot of the quilt-covered bed. The bedroom was sweet with tiny rosebud wallpaper softening the walls. White ruffled curtains framing a large bay window seat rippled in the wind.

The view was stunning. Jagging mountains dominated the horizon, and the sky was the bluest she'd ever seen. Deep greens of trees and the neat rows of a garden gave way to white fencing beyond. And, she realized, as she eased onto the window seat's plump cushion, to Caleb.

Tucked in the shade of the stable, he was brushing the white horse. He hadn't noticed her and she didn't seem able to look away. There was something about him that felt as calming to her as the gentle breeze through the open window. It wasn't every day a girl got to round up runaway horses with a handsome—and kind—cowboy. It was a new experience for her. She couldn't help wondering about her brother and sisters in the family photograph. This was probably the way they'd grown up, with visits here and adventures on those horses and family meals made with vegetables grown in the garden.

Her grandmother's words replayed in her mind. *Don't think because you didn't grow up here, that you were out of my thoughts or my heart, because that wouldn't be true.*

Those words had meant a lot. For the first time in her life, the haze of unhappiness from her childhood felt far away and she could see clearly. The meeting with her grandmother had gone well—her initial worries were over. Now, there was the rest of the family to meet—tomorrow. For now, she was grateful to have the time to get to know Mary.

She checked the time on the way out the door. She wanted to make sure she helped her grandmother in the kitchen. Rose-scented air greeted her as she skipped down the steps. Caleb's baritone carried on the hot wind. He was calling her name. Still brushing the white horse's sleek coat, he flashed his dimpled grin. He raised a hand, gesturing her over.

He was a kind man and hard not to like. So she headed his way through the fragrant flower garden ripe with full blooms of colorful roses then along the edge of the vegetable garden.

He came up to the fence, his Stetson shading his granite features. "Things look like they're goin' pretty well."

"Better than I'd let myself hope."

"You must have awful low hopes as a general rule. You said you talked to Mary on the phone. You had to suspect she'd be as nice in person."

"Yes, but you just never know how things are going to turn out."

"You've got a smile on your face. That about says it all."

She shrugged, not wanting to talk about her feelings. She was a private person, Caleb got that. He was pretty private himself. Her gaze went behind him to the mare standing in the shade of the horse barn. There was a look of wistfulness there. "I hope they don't get out again. What if you hadn't been around to catch them?"

"Ah, but you see, that's the fun part of the game for Malia. She wants me to know she can get out any old time she wants. But what she really wants is for me to chase her. She loves to run. And to win."

"I see. You indulge her by letting her outrun the pickup."

"Now, don't you let her hear that, or it's gonna make her cranky." Caleb checked over his shoulder at the mare who'd pricked her ears and narrowed her eyes. "Don't let her fool you. She understands English about as well as I do. Maybe better, since she's got nothing more to do than to stand around all day pondering it."

That made Lauren smile. "You seem to know her pretty well. I hear from my grandmother that she's known you all of your life."

"That about sums it up. My family has known hers for generations. I spent summers out here, until my grandparents downsized to a small house in town and I bought the place from them. I keep an eye on Mary's place, take care of her horses, that kind of thing. I keep my own horse here, he likes the company. You've already met him. Here he comes."

The brown and white paint pushed up to the fence, sniffing the air in hopes for any kind of treat. He pressed right up against the fence and reached over it with his long neck.

"I'm used to horses on television." Lauren took one step back. "I didn't know they were so big in real life."

"They look even bigger when you're on one of 'em, looking down."

"I believe you."

She wasn't scared, he realized as she hung back, just uncertain. His fiancée, Jayna, had been petrified of horses, and that had been a problem. One of many that had been impossible to overcome. He ran a hand down his boy's neck. "Hey, you big lug, listen up and use your manners for the lady. Stop nosing around for food, Leo."

Leo took exception to that and gave a head toss, his silky brown mane rippling handsomely. A charmer from the day he was foaled, the gelding preened, arching his neck for the lady watching him. The horse was determined to impress her.

It seemed to work, although by the instant adoration in her eyes, clearly Lauren was soft-hearted. "He's gorgeous."

"Sure, and he knows it, too. Look at him showing off. He's winking at you."

"He's cheeky. You taught him that, didn't you?"

"Sure did. I suppose there weren't horses where you grew up."

"The kind on the merry-go-round. As a little girl, I always wanted a horse. I read every book with a horse in it. Watched everything I could find on TV. It was just a phase, I guess."

"It's a phase I never grew out of."

"It must be nice."

That made him wonder about her life *and* what she thought of him. There was a polish to her that made him guess she was right at home among skyscrapers and jam-packed streets and people everywhere. He was country through and through, but he understood. He'd liked living in Seattle, even if he'd felt hemmed in now and then.

Her sleek golden hair fluttered around her sweetheart's face, framing it perfectly. In the mellow evening sunshine, she looked kissed by innocence. Like everything sweet and good in the world.

Not that he ought to be noticing that. Or the graceful way she moved, like the sunlight itself, with an unconscious poise that made her seem completely out of place in the rugged rural countryside of central Montana. His chest ached a little, but he couldn't say why. Only that he couldn't seem to look away as she reached up to stroke Leo's nose. The gelding leaned into Lauren's touch, as if he'd already made up his mind about the newcomer.

Yeah, that's what he thought, too. Caleb tried to clear the ache out of his chest with a good deep breath of warm summer air, but it didn't work.

"Well," she said as she took a step back. "If I want to help with dinner, I'd best get going."

Maybe it was the longing look as she gazed at the horse or simply his curiosity about her, but the words tumbled across his tongue before he could stop them. "Come meet me out here tomorrow morning and I'll take you riding with me."

"I'd love that, but there's one problem."

"Let me guess. You don't know how to ride."

"Yes, and it's a rather huge problem."

"Nope. I can teach you to ride in five minutes."

"That's a fib. Flaw number one." Why wasn't she surprised? Lauren kept backing away, because it was safer. Even a man as awesome as Caleb Stone had his flaws. "I know it takes more than five minutes to learn to ride. All those horse books and movies, remember?"

"Well, I didn't say you'd ride like an expert, but in five minutes I can have you on the back of a horse riding around the corral."

"Overconfidence. Flaw number two."

"Hey, are you keeping count or something?"

"Me? Of course not. It's habit, that's all." Maybe it was better to escape while she could, before she had to explain that. But maybe—down deep—she wanted to get away before she thought too much. She couldn't let herself think that he was as great as he seemed, as she seemed to want him to be.

So she left the man with his horse awash in sunlight. And tried to turn her thoughts to other things as she hurried back to the path. She didn't look back, although she could feel him watching after her, even when she'd disappeared around the garden patch and hurried out of his sight.

She climbed the porch steps, wondering if there was a man on earth a woman could truly depend on? She sure hoped so. But people let you down. Especially men. That was a proven fact in life—both in hers and in her mother's.

Although the kitchen door was open, the screen door was closed. The mesh screen offered a view into the big sunny room with kettles boiling on the stove and a table scooted up to the wide picture window. Touches of lace were everywhere—delicate and handmade and frilly, they graced the windows, lay across the honeyed wood of the table and framed the snapshots on the walls. The room was like something out of an old television show as safe and as welcoming as home should be.

Lauren rapped her knuckles gently on the wooden frame of the screen door.

Mary peered around the inside archway. "Lauren. Come in, dear. I couldn't help noticing you were talking to Caleb. He's a very nice boy, don't you think?"

Uh oh. Here it came. Lauren closed the screen door behind her, wincing at the look of hope shining on her grandmother's sweet face. "Yes, Caleb seems very nice, but he's not my type."

"Really? You mean you're not looking for a responsible, dependable, kind, smart man with old-fashioned values?" A challenge sparkled in Mary's gentle smile.

"Sorry, I'm not looking for that. Not at all." Lauren hoped she was able to cover up her real emotions, feelings that were too complicated to get into. "I'm more of a solo kind of girl."

"That's too bad you feel that way. My marriage was one of the greatest things in my life." Mary's smile changed and the look in her eyes did, too. "Being his wife, sharing his life, why, it was the greatest privilege."

That was something Lauren couldn't understand. She couldn't imagine trusting anyone so much or letting anyone get that close. She held back her reasons why: the up-and-down relationships of her mother's; the short and stormy marriages; the quest for the next husband, none of whom could possibly have been described as great.

"I don't really want to be a wife." It was the closest thing to the truth she could say, the only thing that was easy. Everything else was too personal. Too painful. She hadn't come all this way to share that with her grandmother.

"Don't want to be a wife?" Mary looked truly confused. "Whatever do you mean? You don't want a husband? A family? Love in your life?"

What did she say to a woman whose life was as removed from her reality as a fifties sitcom? "I'm happy with the way things are right now."

"I see." Mary studied Lauren for a long silent moment and in the stillness between them, the evening light shone a deep-hued rose. The room was painted by it; Mary seemed transformed by it.

Lauren could see the windows awash with the tone, the entire sky beyond a translucent turquoise and the clouds a neon pink. It was unreal, like a filter over a camera's lens changing the hues of the world. That's what it was like. The streaks of last light fractured as the sun lowered beneath the craggy rugged mountain peaks. The neon pink remained, lighting the underbellies of the long stretch of clouds. The sky turned a navy-purple tone, darkening as the moments passed.

"I'll leave well enough alone, then," Mary said as twilight deepened in the room. "You can't blame a grandmother for hoping. I want all my grandchildren married and settled and happy in life."

Lauren knew that Mary meant well. Maybe if she'd grown up here in the gentle shadow of the breathtaking Rocky Mountains with the love of this sunny, kind woman, she would be different. More trusting. Looking for love and marriage and happily-ever-after like a heroine in a romantic movie. It was a nice thought.

"It's just that Caleb has just come out of a

bad breakup." Mary traced a finger over the words on the cover of a photo album. "He's a good man and he deserves to find the right young woman. Someone nice."

"Wait, you hardly know me. How do you know I'm nice?" She'd meant it to lighten the mood, but Mary's face fell.

"My dear, why of course I know you." Mary stood, coming after her, with her hands held out. "I've loved you forever."

Mary brushed her free hand over the wisps of Lauren's hair and tucked them behind her ear, as one would do to a small child. "I hope that you and I can get to know each other well before you head back to your life. I want you to find what you've come for."

Pain jerked through the core of her being. "I haven't come for anything. I'm not like my mother. I vowed long ago not to be like her. You don't know that, I know, but it's true. I didn't come here to get something."

"Oh, yes you did," Mary said, pressing a kiss to her cheek. "And it's what I need, too. Thank you for coming when I asked. Forgive me, but it's getting late and my old bones are tired. Thank you for coming all this way. I wanted to meet you while I can remember."

This she said with a smile. Shadows clung beneath her vibrant eyes and cut deep brackets around her mouth. In this light, it would be easy to believe Mary wasn't well. Affection for this dear lady warmed Lauren through, but she also felt concern. "Are you all right?"

"Yes, dear. I'm as right as rain. But I'm not getting any younger." Mary turned to the stove to check on the boiling kettles. She poked a fork into a potato inside one of the pots. "I guess none of us are. I gathered up a few family photo albums. They're on the edge of the counter, right by the table. You missed so many good years, maybe this will help you understand when you meet your brother and sisters tomorrow."

Okay, that idea made her seriously anxious. So much could go wrong. She tried to remind herself that so much could go right, too. She would be the outsider either way—and that was a role she was used to.

But this feeling of, well, connectedness was new.

There was understanding bright in Mary's eyes. "Well, the potatoes are done. Let me get them drained and the pot roast on the table, then you and I will catch up. I want to hear all about your life. Your college classes. Your drive here. Meeting Caleb. Everything."

It was hard to say no to that. Lauren went to help put the meal on the table.

Chapter Four

There was nothing like a Montana morning. Caleb liked to watch the sunrise come as quietly as an answered prayer. The webby shadows of darkness giving way to the gray-purple that came before dawn. By the time the promise of the sun was aglow, backlighting the rugged peaks of the Bridger Range, Caleb was climbing out of his truck with his travel mug of hot tea in hand and greeting the horses at the gate. Malia was the alpha horse, first to the rail and nipping to keep the others in line.

"Be nice," he reminded her as he hauled

the bucket of oats with him. Leaving his mug on a fence post, he spread out the molasses-sweetened oats in the long feed trough and the horses dug in. The sound of their crunching drowned out the lark song sweet in the fresh air. He gave Leo a welcoming pat and reached for his steaming mug.

As he took a sip, he scanned Mary's spread—the home, gardens, pool, patios and carriage house. He didn't really mean to notice, but the little guest home's windows were open and the curtains drawn back, as if welcoming the day. Lauren was up? He couldn't put his thumb on why that surprised him, but it did.

It was Jayna, that's why. He knew better, but he'd painted city girls with the same slightly bitter brushstroke, mostly because it hurt less that way. Wounds of the heart took a long time to mend and sometimes they didn't heal over as completely as one might like. Still, he had to get over it. It had been almost two years, long enough to put all of it, even the scars, behind him.

He savored the crisp taste of the cinnamon tea and tried to let the morning's peace spill into him. But he couldn't seem to take his gaze from Lauren's cottage. Maybe it was her presence he sensed, since a few moments later there she was, wading toward him through the knee-high grass.

Dressed in jeans and a pink T-shirt, she looked as refreshing as the morning and as innocent as the wildflowers at her feet. Not that he ought to be noticing those things, either.

"Good morning, Caleb." Her soft alto was hushed as she came nearer. "You're a very early riser, too?"

"Guilty. Besides, the horses appreciate being fed first thing in the morning. How'd the evening go with your grandmother?"

"Wonderful."

"You say that with relief. Like you were really worried."

"In my experience, you can never tell about people, especially right when you meet them. I'm not the most trusting person, I guess. But we had such a good time looking through old photo albums. It was past midnight before we knew it."

"I reckon Mary loved sharing those photographs—and the time—with you."

"Oh, I'm the lucky one. She is nothing short of amazing. I don't know how Mom stole money from such a nice woman. And the family jewelry and heaven knows what else."

"You figure everyone looks at you and sees her?"

"I would. I never answered birthday cards or sent a thank-you for Christmas gifts. I didn't know I'd gotten them." Her unconscious shrug seemed to dismiss the issue.

He could tell there was a lot of pain there. "I suppose there was money in those birthday cards and pawnable items in those Christmas boxes?"

"That's my guess, too. I was too little to know the difference and when I was older, everyone here had written Mom off for good and me along with her. Not that I blame her. Mom has a real destructive streak."

"That's why you don't have much to do with her?"

"I left home for the college dorm and didn't look back. There wasn't anything to go back to. Just a basement apartment with security bars on the windows. Nothing like what you're used to here."

There it was, he saw the shadows darken her eyes. Past hurts. He knew how that was. Yet she waved them away with an unconscious gesture.

He couldn't help liking her. She was nice. And she'd been on his mind through the evening. Here she was standing before him with a wistful expression, looking at the mountains and pastures and horses. The promise he'd made stood between them and he felt it sorely. "Are you ready for your riding lesson?"

"Now?"

"Sure. I usually saddle up before I have to head in to work. Nothing like a morning ride to start your day off right."

"What do you do for a living?"

"I'm a town cop." He watched her eyes widen and she took a step back. "What, you don't like policemen?"

"I don't have the best association with them." *Great, now he thinks I have a record.* Lauren rolled her eyes. She was getting off on the wrong foot with this man. One thing she really didn't like was looking back into the past. "When I was little, Mom had a hard time keeping up with the rent. We were given notice of eviction a few times. Court ordered."

"That's rough."

When he could have been judgmental, he sounded kind. Somehow that was harder to accept. "There are worse things in the world. Like pandemics. Wide-scale starvation."

"Those things would be rougher."

"Exactly. In the scheme of things, it wasn't so bad."

The compassion in his eyes and—again—the kindness in his voice made her like him even more. Against her will, apparently. "A cop, huh?"

"Yep. I try to be one of the good ones."

"I don't doubt that." She could see him in her mind's eye, all suited up in his uniform, upholding the law with that kindness of his. And compassion. Her heart tugged with an emotion she would not acknowledge. Back to the horses, which were a much safer subject. "Can you really teach me to ride in five minutes?"

"Absolutely." He'd parked his truck nearby and he was already reaching into the back. "See the brown mare?"

"You mean the *tallest* horse?"

"That's the one."

"You're going to give me the biggest horse, knowing that I'll probably fall off and land on my hind end in the dirt?" She was laughing, though. He had to be teasing her. "You're going to give me the short one to learn to ride on, right?"

"Oh, I see what you're saying, city girl. You're worried about falling off a horse. Well, falling is certain. Getting back up is what separates the men from the boys. Or, in your case, the women from the girls. But that doesn't sound right."

"No, it doesn't. I think you're making fun of a city girl, Mr. Stone."

"I'd never be disrespectful to any woman, no matter where she hailed from."

I will not be charmed by him, she thought. Liking him a little tiny bit was one thing. Letting herself feel more was another. "And what about the falling part? I've never realized how far it is from the back of the horse to the ground. It looks a lot farther than I've ever imagined. Maybe it's smart *not* to get back up."

She was like the sunlight—quietly cheerful. Caleb was smiling, too, without knowing it, chuckling right along with her as he hauled the bridles out of the truck bed. She was all right. "Tasha is a gentle giant. You shouldn't fall off. Much. Unless…how's your sense of balance? If it's terrible, you *might* fall off no matter which horse I sit you on."

"I didn't realize how much I'd have to trust you. I'm at your mercy. Maybe I'd better rethink this horse-riding thing."

But her eyes were smiling again and she radiated anticipation. He thought about what she'd told him, about her mother not being reliable enough to pay the rent regularly enough to keep a stable home for her child. "Hey, you can trust me. I'm an upstanding sort. C'mon, city girl, let's get you up on your first horse."

"As long as I stay up." She followed him, climbing through the fence's rails. How could it be possible that the horse got bigger with every step she took?

"It only hurts if you fall, Lauren. Otherwise, it's a piece of cake. Don't worry, we'll go slow. Hey, Tasha girl." He held the big bay by a halter strap so he could slip the bridle on and buckle it securely. When he was done, Tasha leaned into his touch for a gentle stroke. "You feel like going for a run, girl?"

Lauren stepped into the horse's shadow and her heart stopped on the word *run*. "I thought wc were going to start slow."

"What happened to trusting me?" Caleb's words were lighthearted, but the look on his face was not. He was iron-strong dependability all the way. "First we walk, then we run. You'll love it."

"I hope so. My expectations are pretty high."

"Don't worry. There's nothing like riding a horse. The experience will surpass your every expectation."

Wouldn't that be a new trend in her life? Lauren was close enough to the mare that she could breathe in her warm, friendly scent. "Hi, girl."

The mare eyed her with what Lauren hoped was a friendly look. She gave a snort and tried to grab the hem of Lauren's shirt with her big teeth.

"Uh, she won't bite me, right?"

"She's just friendly. Give her nose a stroke or two. I'll leave you two to get acquainted. I'll be right back."

"Wait." But he was already moving away, releasing his hold on the leather bridle.

Tasha looked even more gigantic as she stepped forward with hooves that suddenly looked able to crush Lauren's feet. "Uh, how do I get acquainted with a horse?"

"You talk to her." He said that as if it was perfectly natural to have a one-sided conversation.

The trouble was, Tasha seemed to be expecting something. She took a harder grip with her teeth on Lauren's hem and shook her head. When the mare stomped her front foot, the earth gave a tiny tremble.

"Hi, pretty girl." Lauren ran her fingertips down the white stripe on the mare's long nose and the sun-warmed velvet feel surprised her. Tasha was so sleek. "You're going to go easy on me, right, since I'm a beginner?"

Tasha released her hold on the shirt and

raised her head so high, she easily snorted the crown of Lauren's head. That's when Lauren realized that Tasha had spied the pink barrette in her hair. And Tasha wasn't the only one. Horses were approaching from every side, corralling her in and nibbling at her hair. "Uh, Caleb. Help!"

"They sure seem to like you," came his amused grin, which, fortunately, accompanied the approaching crunch of his boots in the grass. "Girls, stop that. It's not candy. Move back, now. Lauren, this'll help."

A gray cowboy hat plopped onto her head, shading her eyes from the sun and hiding the pink barrette from sight. Caleb, at her side, seemed to make this new adventure feel just right. Comfortable. Safe.

How about that? She actually felt at ease with a man. Probably because her grandmother had sung his praises all evening. The great things he did for her, without any thought of compensation. How responsible he was. How good.

There was good in everyone, she reminded herself. But lessons learned had taught her there was bad, too, and that's what hurt a person. She had to keep up her guard.

Still, it was hard to keep up her guard when the man in question had just come to her rescue. A few of the horses backed off and there was Caleb, weaving his fingers together to offer her a step up.

"You ready?" Not only was there a light challenge in the crook of his grin but also a steady burning reassurance that made it seem as if everything would turn out perfect.

"As ready as I'll ever be." She eyed Tasha's back, which looked much wider and higher than she'd ever imagined a horse's back to be. "Are you sure I don't need a saddle?"

"I'm sure, city girl. Put your foot in my hand—no, the other one. That's right. Grab hold of her mane. And you're gonna swing your leg over. Take care not to give her a kick in the backside. Lift your foot all the way over."

Tasha seemed to be worried about that, too, as she swung her head around to keep an eye on the goings-on. She really did seem like a nice horse, Lauren thought. Just the kind of horse she'd always wanted as a little girl.

"Don't worry," she told the mare. "I won't kick you for the world."

Caleb lifted her and up she went. Just like that she was on Tasha's back. She was careful not to bump her shoe against Tasha's side, either, as she tried to adjust to the rather strange sensation.

"This isn't like sitting on a chair." For one thing, the mare felt so *alive*. Lauren felt the ripple of muscle and strength, and she had to adjust her balance when the horse shifted a little and tossed her head. Definitely a weird sensation. Probably something similar to standing on the top pole of a sailboat in mid ocean. Plus, the ground seemed a mile away down there. And the grass, which was soft when she'd been earthbound, looked as hard as brick.

Falling off would definitely be a very bad idea. She gripped Tasha's mane with both hands and wished she'd talked Caleb into saddling the horse. Tasha's coat was like expensive velvet and it wouldn't take much to go sliding right off.

But Caleb had a steadying hold on her

ankle. "It's a whole different perspective from up there, isn't it?"

"Yes." She let out a breath and realized once the initial panic was over, being horseback was very pleasant. Like touching a little dream.

Caleb released his grip on her ankle and she was really doing it, really on the back of a beautiful mare. With the wide meadow fenced in and the morning wind bathing her face, it felt like anything was possible.

Caleb had hopped up onto Leo's back and came to gather up Tasha's reins. With quiet competence, he handed them to Lauren, and she noticed, this close, that his eyes weren't as dark as she'd first thought. His brown irises were threaded with bronze and green. She could also see the freshly shaven angle of his jaw.

Not that she should be noticing those things. It wasn't as if she could possibly be interested, right?

But as he showed her how to hold the reins in one hand, she noticed more about him than what he was saying about riding. His nose was very straight and not too big, just right for his strongly angled face. And while he was a big man, he was athletic and moved easily. He laid his gloved hand over hers, showing her how to hold on to Tasha's coarse mane. He seemed so self-assured, Lauren didn't want to point out that she didn't know how a handful of horse hair was going to keep her from toppling right off.

"That's it, now gentle pressure against her sides with your heel," he instructed. "Not like they show in the movies with a kick. You do that and she'll either take off at a dead gallop or turn around and bite your ankle."

"You said she didn't bite."

"Mostly she doesn't." He winked.

Yeah, he thought he was so charming. Refusing to encourage such behavior, even if it *was* warranted, she lifted her chin a notch and carefully pressed the heels of her sneakers to Tasha's sides.

The mare moved forward into a smooth walk. Yikes, it was not what she expected. It was a little like whiplash, but after a few of Tasha's steps, Lauren started to get the horse's rocking motion.

Wow, it wasn't so hard. She threw Caleb a

grin, ready to say "Look at the city girl now," but she slipped to the side. Okay, maybe she was getting a little ahead of herself. She kept sliding and Caleb was there, taking her by the elbow to steady her.

"That's right." His grip was an unyielding support. "I won't let you fall."

She believed him. Of course, he was talking about her falling off the horse. But what surprised her was the part that wanted to believe in a man. That there was a man in existence who would never let her fall. In any way, in any circumstance, ever. A surprise? Definitely. She didn't know how that wish could have survived her childhood, but it had—just a little bit.

"See? You're riding." Caleb released her, although he kept Leo at Tasha's side. "It took a few minutes and you're doing great. What do you think of riding?"

"Fantastic." She still felt as if she were going to topple off any second, but it was getting better. Her sense of balance was improving and if she relaxed instead of sitting board stiff, then Tasha's rolling gait moved through her and they were in sync. Sure, it wasn't championship riding, but hey, she hadn't fallen yet.

Caleb, of course, sat astride like a pro. "Look at that sunrise. It heartens a person."

Maybe that's exactly what she needed. When she looked up—still trying to keep her balance and slipping a little—she'd never seen anything as breathtaking as the purple mountains rimming the horizon in every direction, polished with the sheen of the golden sunrise. It felt as if she'd landed in a completely different world. Gone were the crowded streets and the search for a parking spot, the standing in line, the people, the noise and the traffic congestion everywhere.

Her troubles seemed just as far away, a distant memory. Working long hours on her feet. Studying late into the night. The thousand things to do she could never keep up on. Making her rent. Stretching every penny. Keeping up her grades for the scholarship she was on. She loved her life; but she hadn't realized how good a vacation—a break away—could be.

"It is heartening," she agreed. "It's so

grand, it makes you feel as if anything is possible. As if you're a whole new person."

"True. It's a refreshing way to start the day."

"I can see why you live here, even if there aren't any malls close by." She didn't say more, but studied the roll of land and the amber, grass-scented air and the peace of the morning, as if she could find an answer there.

She felt how different she would have been if she'd grown up here, in this place of wide-open spaces and horse pastures and Mary's loving kindness. Caleb seemed so rooted, steady and confident and honest, all in a way that said he was at peace with himself and with his place in this little corner of the world.

She could not say the same, nor why this revelation made her sad on such a sweet, bright morning.

They approached the river winding through the meadow. Cottonwoods had dug into the bank and the horses stopped in their sparse shade.

She drank in the serenity. She'd never been near such stillness. It wasn't the ocean on a clear morning, but this was grand in its own way. A sense of hope began to whisper in her soul like the breeze through the wild grasses. Yes, she definitely needed this trip, for more reasons than she could count.

"A week ago, I never would have imagined being in this beautiful place riding a horse. A *horse*."

"It's my kind of fun, but then I'm not a symphony-going, young-urban-professional kind of a guy."

"There's a lot to be said for cowboys." She tugged the brim of her hat a little higher. "Thanks for this, Caleb."

"No problem. I don't mind sharing my morning with a city slicker. As long as you don't mind sharing yours with a country guy."

That made her smile. "Not at all. Of course, maybe the real draw for me is the horse." She flashed him a smile, gently teasing—something she never did. One of the reins slipped from her fingers.

"Let me." He leaned in his saddle to rescue the leather strap. "You know, Tasha has taught more than one McKaslin sister how to ride."

"Really?" Worry crept across her forehead

and dug in along her rosebud mouth as she took the recovered rein from him. She was careful not to brush her fingers against his. "Which sisters?"

"Katherine, I know for sure. Aubrey, I think. I'm not sure about Ava. She didn't have the best luck when it came to horses. And Rebecca, she's the stepsister."

"Because my dad remarried." Shadows crept into her eyes and she bowed her head, the wide brim of the Stetson hiding the expression on her face.

"He married a nice lady with two girls of her own. The youngest is about your age, I think. You'll probably meet them today."

"Probably." The knuckles on her hand turned white.

It had to be hard coming back, not knowing for sure if you were welcome. "It'll be okay. I know it."

Her hands remained tight on the reins. "From your lips to God's ears. I've always wanted a sister in my life."

"Now you have five of them, counting the steps."

"I hope I like them. I want them to like me."

His throat lodged tight. He couldn't say why or what he was feeling, but he could read her earnestness. Maybe it was time for a change in subject to get her mind off her worries. "You see that house way over there on that rise?"

"You mean the only house I can see for what looks like miles?"

He chuckled. "It must seem that way to someone used to folks every which way you look, but my spread is about a quarter of a mile away."

"You call that next door?" Gentle amusement brightened her violet-blue eyes. "It must have been nice growing up around here. Quiet, but nice."

"There isn't a better way in my opinion. All this open space. Lots to do. I was never bored."

"Really?" Lauren tried to imagine what a person could do in all these grassy fields and forested foothills. No shopping, no theaters, no centers of learning. "I caught a glimpse of the city from the freeway and it didn't look very big. What do you do for fun, besides ride horses?"

"Oh, like I needed to go into town to find something to do? Is that what you mean?" He quirked one brow in a challenge.

Goodness, had she offended him? "I was just wondering. I grew up with kids everywhere. There was always something to do, jumping rope or hopscotch or, when I was older, playing basketball or going down the street to the youth center. That's all. If you grew up here, it would be hard to step outside your front door and find enough kids to play a game of baseball."

"True. But then, I'm not much of a baseball player. Besides, what could be more fun than this?" He grinned.

He did have a point. Horses were pretty cool. "Why do I get the feeling that you aren't as small town as you want me to believe?"

He knuckled back his Stetson. "I spent a few years out of state. Thought there weren't enough opportunities here and, like most of the kids I'd grown up with, thought I'd find them in a bigger place."

"Where did you go?"

"Seattle. It's a nice city, don't get me wrong, but the opportunities aren't better, just different. You've got to decide what your priorities are and what you want. For me, I figured out that I liked this lifestyle. I didn't want to trade it for better pay and more choices. Besides, if I want culture, all I've got to do is sit down with my volume of Shakespeare."

"I can't picture it. Maybe it's the cowboy hat."

"Maybe. What do you do to make a living?"

"I have an internship at a financial investment company. Of course that's for no pay, just school credit. I also have a job to pay the rent. I have a roommate and that helps cut some of the costs."

"Sounds like you have a pretty busy life."

"Sometimes too busy, but I manage to keep everything together, mostly. Until I get through my master's program I'm just taking one day at a time and being glad for that."

"That's pretty much what I do, too." Caleb reined Leo around. His chest felt all wadded up and troubled, but he couldn't say why. The morning was pure serenity and sharing it with a nice pretty lady was no hardship.

Maybe it was the lady. Maybe it was from trying to picture her student lifestyle. He knew it wasn't an easy row to hoe. She was nice and that made the tangle in his chest ache a little.

As they headed back, he kept her in his sight. She looked lovely with the wind tousling her hair and the mellow golden sheen of the light falling across her. Beneath the Stetson's wide brim, her face shone with wonder and delight as she leaned forward to whisper something to Tasha. Apparently pleased with the affection, the mare preened, and that knot in him yanked a little tighter.

The trouble was, he didn't want to like Lauren. Not even a little bit.

She turned to him when they reached the white rail fencing, where they'd first started out. "This might be the best morning I've ever had."

"Surely not the best."

"At least that I can remember." Lauren hated that the ride was over, but she knew Caleb had a work day ahead and she had— oh, thinking of it made her stomach clench into a hard fist, an equal mix of excitement and abject terror. Meeting her family. So much could go wrong, so much could go right. She was equally scared of both. One would make her mother right and the other, it was the unknown. She wanted a family. She also didn't want to get hurt.

So far, so good, right? Maybe this morning was a good sign. Maybe the meeting will go so well, she would be glad she'd come.

Maybe, just maybe, it would change her life.

"I'm glad that you had such a good time. You did a pretty good job for a city girl." Caleb had slid down to the ground and was unbuckling Leo's bridle.

"I didn't fall once."

"Better than I did my first time out. It would be my pleasure to give you another lesson tomorrow, if you're up for it."

"Are you sure? I'd love it."

"Are you an early riser by nature?" Caleb hung the bridle on the top rail and came toward her.

"Mornings are my favorite time of day."

"Mine, too. Good. Then we'll meet thirty

minutes earlier and go for a longer ride. How about it?"

"Sounds perfect."

Caleb held out his hands and she placed her palms against his. So warm and unyielding. He helped her slide safely to the ground. Her feet hit the earth and she felt the jolt in her soul. In that moment, she saw understanding in Caleb's dark eyes and sensed it in the air between them.

"You're worried about these people you're about to meet," he said. "You're afraid that they'll let you down, too. That they won't want you, the way your mom didn't really want you."

"H-how did you know?"

"I lost my mom when I was eight. My grandparents raised me. And I know how there's a place that's always missing the love you should have been given. But it'll be all right. Trust me."

Standing in his shadow, with him towering above her so that he was all she could see of the world, she believed him. It seemed as if anything was possible.

Then he tipped his hat, like a Western

legend and moved away. While he unbuckled Tasha's bridle, Lauren tried to gather up the scattered pieces of her heart, not sure what she was feeling about this man, when the sound of tires on the gravel driveway caught her attention. A beige sedan was pulling up to the far side of the garage, to one of the outbuildings.

"Looks like you get to test out my theory." Caleb gestured toward that beige car. "That's one of your sisters now."

Chapter Five

Her sister. Lauren looked at the slender blond woman climbing out of the car, a woman who had the same shade of blond hair, the same blue eyes and face shape. *Her sister.* Lauren's heart stalled. As she stumbled forward, somehow her wobbly knees worked and she got through the gate Caleb was opening for her.

"C'mon." His baritone was a comforting rumble against her ear. "I'll introduce you to Aubrey."

Aubrey. Her mind groped through a sudden haze. Why was Caleb's nod of encouragement all she noticed? "Aubrey's one of the twins?"

"That's right."

The woman—her sister—was hurrying her way. She'd left her car door open and it was dinging away; she must have left the keys in the ignition.

"You're Lauren. You have to be. Right?"

Suddenly there was no distance between them and Aubrey had thrown her arms around her in a warm, welcoming embrace. Welcoming. There was no question, no judgment, nothing but honest acceptance. Lauren stepped back, swiping her eyes, her vision blurred. Her mother's prediction and her own fears vanished, just like that.

"I can't believe this." Aubrey held tight to Lauren's hand. "You're really here. After all this time. I never thought—" She took a gulp and there were tears in her eyes. "Welcome back to us. Do you remember me at all?"

There was an image, just beyond her reach, taking form and shape in the black places of her memory. A flash of sunlight reflecting off the side passenger door. The blur of the big round faces of the sunflowers hanging heavily, ripe with seeds. The flicker of the white picket fence that divided the backyard from the alley. She remembered the sound of her own cries. A flash of children's faces in the backyard before they'd been gone to her. "It's all a blur. I wish I could remember more."

"I have never forgotten you. I can't believe this. I saw Gran yesterday at the bookstore and she didn't say a word. Not a single word. When did you get in?"

"Yesterday evening."

"She was keeping this secret! It's a good thing I decided to come out bright and early and get some work done in my studio—I do ceramics—but like I want to do that now? I don't think so." Aubrey was tugging her in the direction of the kitchen door, all joy. "We are going to go surprise Gran right now. I want her to know her plan to surprise us with you has failed. Caleb, are you coming?"

Lauren realized he'd retreated, leaving her with her sister. *Her sister.* Aubrey held her so tight, there was no way she could escape even if she wanted to. After all this time on her own, spending holidays alone, she had a sister. Sisters. There it was, hope rising up through the dark void of her memories. She held on to Aubrey's hand a little more tightly.

Across the driveway, Caleb lifted his hand to his hat brim. "I've got to get to work. You two have fun catching up. Lauren, I'll see you later."

His gaze met hers and it was as reassuring as a touch. As if he was saying to her, "See, I told you it would be all right." And he'd been right. She should have had more faith in him.

She let Aubrey tug her up the porch steps and still she couldn't look away completely from the man. Caleb was watching them, watching her, his face shadowed beneath his Stetson, his expression inscrutable.

The hinges of the screen door rasped and squeaked, and she tumbled into the living room behind Aubrey. Lauren lost sight of him then. But she didn't lose the sense of peace and support he'd given to her.

A few hours later, Lauren leaned toward the front seats of Aubrey's car and squinted through the glare on the windshield. There it was, the family's bookstore. Her brother and younger stepsister worked there; they were probably watching for Aubrey's sedan through the long, windowed storefront. Aubrey had made the call from Gran's kitchen phone to announce they were all coming. So more introductions were ahead. The weight of the past punched at her temples like a professional boxer's gloves.

"I was so stunned I almost locked my keys in the car. Me!" Aubrey was saying into her cell as she pulled into a parking spot. Mature maples offered shade and relief from the blazing midday sun. "We're here, so I'll see you in a few."

"Lauren, dear," Gran said from the front passenger seat. "Don't you worry about this. I hadn't wanted to spring everyone on you all at once, but I guess the cat's out of the bag."

"I guess so, Gran. Don't worry. I was going to meet them tonight anyway. This just gives me more time with everyone." She was starting to feel optimistic. It was a new feeling and she liked it.

Lauren unbuckled her seat belt and noticed that Gran seemed to be having a little trouble with her's. Lauren leaned forward to reach between the front seats and over the console. "Do you need some help with that?"

"No, dear. It's just that these buckles are all

so different." The older woman's voice rang sweet and true.

Lauren watched the worry dig into Aubrey's face and realized there was more going on here—and perhaps more to her grandmother's invitation. Gran's words came to mind again. *I wanted to meet you while I can remember.* Even if she was all right now, time took a toll on everyone. Lauren remembered the fragile feel of her grandmother's arm in her own when they'd hugged in greeting last night.

I'm so glad I came, Lauren thought. Her own purposes, her own hopes for coming no longer mattered so much. This kind, gentle woman did.

So she hurried out of the car to open her grandmother's door and offered a hand to help her out of the car.

"Why thank you, Lauren." Mary sounded surprised, but pleased. "What do you think of our place?"

Lauren considered it while she closed both car doors. The front of the store stretched across a wide expanse of tall windows that invited the eye right in. She saw colorful displays of sun catchers and wind chimes, of books set around a display, the flash of crystal and the curve of an armchair. The Corner Bookstore was written in tasteful black script across the double glazed front doors. The store was embedded in a larger complex of storefronts. This was where her dad used to work? "It's wonderful."

"My Franklin's parents started the store right before the first World War, and I kept it open when Franklin went off to fight in the Second World War. He made it through Normandy and every battle after and came home to me. Our son was set to take over when we retired, but we lost him in Vietnam. That's when it went to John and your mother. Then Dorrie came along and she worked so hard. She's like a daughter to me. Now, they've passed it on to their children. A real family tradition." Mary lit up with pride. "There's Spence now, dear. Brace yourself, he's wound pretty tight."

Lauren caught the hint of a tall, austere looking man on the other side of the windows, striding swiftly toward the glass doors.

Aubrey closed her car door and over the top

of the roof, she sent a huge look of apology. "We're so sorry for him."

"What do you mean?" Lauren asked, but there was no time for Aubrey's answer.

The door swung open to reveal a tall, wide-shouldered man with perfectly groomed brown hair and piercing blue eyes. His scowl would do a villain justice. This was her brother? Her hopes began to sink. He tossed her a dismissive glance, his upper lip might have lifted up in the corner in a sneer, but she could have imagined it, before he turned his back on her and commandeered their grandmother.

He clearly didn't like her.

"Gran. You shouldn't be surprising us like this." Spence escorted Mary up onto the sidewalk with care. "You should have called me to help if you were having a problem with Linda's daughter."

So, the past wasn't left behind completely. This reaction was what she'd feared when she'd agreed to Mary's invitation to visit. Her mother—there was no accounting for all that she'd put everyone through, Lauren could see that now, for Linda had needed money to help her chase her empty dreams.

Gran seemed distressed. "Spence, you have it all wrong. I hired a private investigator to find Lauren. I thought—"

"You what?" Spence looked outraged.

Lauren pressed her hand to her heart. His anger didn't hurt. She wouldn't let it. That man was her older brother. He looked nothing like the teenager from the family photograph on the cottage's wall. He was harsh and unforgiving and expected the worst of her. What if the others shared his opinion? That old familiar loneliness wrapped around her like a cold wind and she shivered.

"Hey, it's just Spence." Aubrey came close, bringing with her a kindness that made that loneliness less chilly. "He's like that. He was hurt pretty bad when Mom left. He took her abandonment so hard. I don't think he's ever really recovered."

"Neither have I." Lauren saw herself in Spence. She wasn't big and harsh and intimidating, but she was on that path. After a while, loneliness and distrust became a habit;

over the years, that habit became harder to break.

"I need to warn you, before we go in," Aubrey was saying in that gentle, quiet way of hers. "We don't talk about Mom, especially not in front of Spence or Dad. In fact, we don't much talk about her at all, anymore. She didn't want to be a part of our lives and we can't go back and make her want to. She put Dad through a lot, afterward. Maybe you didn't know that."

"No. Mom said terrible things about everyone. I grew up hearing it so often, I guess I halfway b-believed it."

"You were two when she took you. You had no say in it. It wasn't your fault."

"Somehow it feels that way."

Aubrey's hand tightened. "It must have been hard being all alone. At least we all had each other."

It had been hard and it was the understanding of it that connected them.

"C'mon," Aubrey said. "Come meet everyone."

They hadn't taken three steps onto the sidewalk when a loud squealing sound tore through the parking lot from behind them. Lauren turned to see Aubrey's identical image rushing toward her, although this twin was wearing a bright yellow apron smeared with streaks of pink and green, her hair was pulled back in a ponytail and her arms were stretched wide.

"Prepare yourself for Ava," Aubrey warned, but it was too late.

Lauren found herself in a tight hug that would have cut off her air supply had it been any tighter.

"This is so totally awesome!" Ava wouldn't let go. "It's our little baby sister all grown up!"

While she heard Aubrey's laugh and Ava's happy squeal, what she most noticed was how hard Ava held on to her, how happy Aubrey sounded, the overwhelming rush of emotion that jammed in her throat. She was wanted. They were all talking at once, Lauren couldn't listen to all of them, her mind was spinning. The ache in her throat swelled until she couldn't swallow. It was amazing any air got through at all. Gran was standing in the shelter of the doorway, beaming with happiness.

"This is so super-duper," Ava chattered happily. "I saw the car pull in and I couldn't believe my eyes. Even if Aubrey hadn't called, I would have totally known you on sight, Lauren."

"I'm Rebecca, by the way," the youngest girl said when Lauren turned back to the group. Rebecca had that college look to her, the one that Lauren knew so well. "Why am I the last to know these things?"

"You're always out of the loop," Aubrey admonished her gently. "If you'd answer your cell phone—"

"Or your e-mail," Ava added.

"Or checked a single message." A middle-aged, motherly looking woman approached, squeezing past Spence who glowered in front of the store. "You don't know a thing about me, Lauren, but I am so glad to finally meet you. My Rebecca and you are almost the same age."

"This is Dorrie." Aubrey leaned in to explain. "Our stepmom."

Stepmom. Dorrie didn't look like any stepmother Lauren had ever seen before. She radiated maternal caring. She took it upon herself to smooth the flyaway hair from Lauren's blurry eyes. She couldn't tell if she was grateful or wistful that this woman had replaced Mom in the family. She seemed like everything a good mother should be. Everything Lauren had once needed.

"Do you know what I'm going to do?" Dorrie asked as the group hug broke apart. "I'm gonna make my special potato salad for your welcome-home dinner tonight."

"Ooh, and your homemade rolls!" Ava pleaded.

Dorrie laughed. "Yes, dearie, I'll make your favorite rolls. This is a celebration. Our Lauren is back with us."

Not a single word could squeeze past the burning knot in her throat. Overwhelmed, she just stood there in the middle of her family like a robot in sleep mode. But her heart was like a too-full dam and the walls couldn't hold it all. Inside, every wall she'd ever built against the loneliness of her childhood crumbled. The feeling of family—of being wanted—swept every defense away.

"Ooh, I'll make dessert!" Ava spoke loud enough to be heard, because everyone was talking at once. "Something chocolate. Lauren, do you like chocolate?"

She managed to nod but still couldn't speak. She had a family. For the first time in her life.

Lauren had been on his mind all day, but when Caleb saw Spence marching across the driveway in his direction, he figured he knew the reason why. He gave the new gate latch a final twist of the screwdriver.

Malia stuck her head over his shoulder to get a good look at her next challenge.

"You leave it be, you hear me?" he told her with a wink and gathered up his tool bag. He met Spence halfway, dreading every step.

Spence didn't look happy. "You knew about her and you didn't tell me."

"I figured it was Mary's place to tell you."

"How long have we been friends?"

"Since we were kids in school—"

"That's a long time. Secrets. That's not what I'd expect of a longtime friend." It was hurt that echoed in the lower tones of

Spence's voice, although he held himself as if angry.

Caleb was sorry for that, too. "It wasn't my place to get involved."

"I see. Well, if it's not your place, then whose is it? Do you know what I saw today?"

"I don't know. What's got you all worked up?" He dumped his tool bag into the back of his truck.

"Seeing her with Gran. Acting as if she cared for her, taking her by the hand to help her out of the car, but ten to one she's no different than Linda."

"Did you notice Lauren at all? She's nice."

"So are a lot of people. Everyone's got a little nice in them. It's the flip side of that, that's the problem." Spence looked truly troubled. "What about Gran? Have you noticed how scattered she is?"

"Not really."

"Well, look closer. She's forgetting things and hiring private detectives to find long-lost relatives. She's inviting perfect strangers into her home. She's fragile. I'm worried about her welfare."

Caleb looked at his friend and saw the past,

when he was the one with unplaced anger and frustration, fists clenched and jaw clamped so tightly his teeth ached. It was a helpless feeling watching your loved ones face the last part of their lives. He'd been there. "You're worried about Mary. I am, too."

"You don't look like it to me. She's wealthy. She and Grandpop worked hard all their lives and she doesn't deserve to be fleeced by some—"

Caleb knew Spence well enough to guess what was behind his seemingly hard stance. Spence wasn't harsh, not down deep. He'd served on the board of many community organizations, trying to make a difference. He cared. That was the bottom line. But when it came to family wounds, little else could cut deeper or leave such a lasting effect.

Caleb did his best to see that now. "You *did* meet Lauren, right? You said you did, but you're not acting like it."

"Oh, sure. Why shouldn't she come across as nice?"

"If you bothered to get to know her at all, then you'd figure, like I do, that her niceness is more than skin-deep."

"How exactly do you know that? You saw her for a few minutes before Gran got here? It takes more than a few minutes—"

This is where it could get complicated, but Caleb bit the bullet. "The truth is, I offered to teach her to ride. She came out and met me for an early morning horse ride. We kept to the pasture, but she seemed so interested in the horses. Maybe she's a country girl at heart."

"Don't be fooled. Linda raised her. Why wouldn't she be just like her? If she's true to form, she'll get close to Gran, close enough to get her hands on enough goods to pawn or get Gran sympathetic enough to write her a fat check and she'll be gone. Never to be heard of again, if we're lucky." Spence looked away, staring hard at the house, his jaw tight.

Worrying about family could do that to a man. You took care of what was yours. End of story. That's just the way it was. Caleb knew that was all Spence was trying to do, because that's how he lived his life, too. He'd come home to Montana and left his fiancée behind to take care of the grandparents who'd raised him, so he knew a thing or two about what his buddy was going through. "All I'm saying is get to know Lauren first, before you make all these judgments. Judgments are like blinders. You see all right looking straight ahead, but it's the whole picture you gotta take careful note of."

"Yeah, I see what you're saying." Spence seemed to consider that.

Caleb heard a car's faint hum carried on the dry wind. He squinted down the road but couldn't see the car yet. Probably Lauren, he figured. She'd been on his mind all day. Maybe because they'd started the day together in this field, maybe because spending time with her had been nice. He liked her; it was hard not to.

The beige sedan came into sight around the bend in the driveway, kicking up a small plume of dust—Ava's new SUV. Maybe Lauren was with her. The thought of seeing Lauren again lit him up inside and the power of it surprised him.

Spence folded his arms over his chest, staring hard at the approaching car. "I think she's after Gran's money."

"You only think that because of the demands your mother made before the divorce. Lauren didn't have anything to do with that." He remembered how unsure she was, how alone. "Maybe it isn't like you think."

"She's been gone twenty years. Not a word in all this time. No calls, nothing. They're the ones who left us. Why would Gran invite her here?"

"Remember, Lauren was too young at the time to make the choice to leave. She's your sister."

"She's a stranger. If she'd been interested in us, she would have let us know before this." He blew out a frustrated sigh.

"Give it some time and you'll see."

"Anything could happen given enough time. That settles it. I'm hiring a private investigator. You can recommend someone, can't you?"

"I've worked with a few good ones over the years. But it's costly. It'll set you back at least several grand."

"I have it. It's not how I want to spend it, but if it goes toward protecting Gran from someone out to hurt her, then it's money well spent."

"Now, don't jump the gun here. Hiring a P.I. is expensive and not even necessary." Caleb had a clear view of Lauren in the front passenger seat. There was something about her. He thought of her as he'd seen her this morning, brushed with the rosy-golden glow of the new day's sun and looking so happy. She'd talked of putting herself through school.

Spence let out a frustrated huff as the SUV slowed to a stop next to the garage. "You're right. Maybe you could do some preliminary stuff for me. Get a credit check. See if she has a record. That sort of thing. See what that brings up before I dig into my savings to hire a detective."

"Spence, I don't think—"

"You think it's sneaky to have my own sister investigated, don't you?" It wasn't distrust but something deeper that darkened Spence's voice. Worry. Hurt. Who knew? But he sounded sincere. "I'm asking you as my friend. For Gran's sake. You'd do the same in my place, admit it."

"I don't think it's necessary, Spence."

"I don't care. Remember your grandmother before she passed?"

Caleb's heart squeezed at the memory of his gentle grandmother and how trusting she was. She'd been vulnerable after Pop had passed away. It was love, Caleb knew, and this was one way a man showed his love, to protect those he held dear. "I'll do a little legwork for you."

"That's a great relief to me. Thanks."

He could see Lauren through the windshield as the SUV circled into the driveway. She lifted her hand in a little finger wave and he waved back. He was definitely drawn to her. He didn't think Spence's worries had any merit to them. "I think it'll be fine, you'll see," he told Spence.

Spence said nothing and Caleb hoped, in time, his friend would let his guards down enough to see the truth. The SUV pulled to a stop and Lauren climbed out of the passenger seat, turning toward him. He didn't think he'd seen any woman more lovely.

The trouble was, he didn't want to like her.

Chapter Six

Through the kitchen's picture window, Lauren kept noticing Caleb on the porch, busily husking corncobs. She wasn't trying to notice. Her gaze simply kept straying to him. She had enough to occupy her thoughts with her sisters in the kitchen. She should concentrate on helping with the dinner preparations and on her sisters, not on a man. So what if he intrigued her? There was nothing more to it than a simple shared horse-riding experience.

Back to work, Lauren. She dug through the biggest drawer, looking for the beaters for the hand mixer.

"Poor Caleb." Aubrey came to gaze toward the window, too. "Out there with a mountain of ears to husk. He needs help."

"I'll do it!" Ava volunteered from her sitting position on the edge of the counter. Aubrey, as the oldest twin and the one in charge, had banished Ava there to keep her out of the way. "I might as well make myself useful," she argued.

"You brought dessert, that was useful," Aubrey said firmly. "Besides, I'm sure Caleb needs actual help."

"I am corn-husking challenged," Ava agreed cheerfully.

It was strange watching them, because she was still an outsider. She didn't know why everyone chuckled in good-natured amusement when Ava had accidentally dropped the colander of newly picked and washed green beans. They'd flown everywhere, and Aubrey quietly gathered them up and washed them off. There had been no anger and no shouting. At least, that was the only family experience Lauren had to draw on. She liked this way much better.

The sisters worked in easy synchronicity. Lauren felt a step behind, but they didn't mean to make her feel that way.

"I'll take over mashing the potatoes." Aubrey's impressive engagement diamond flashed as she opened a cabinet and grabbed the hand mixer. "I think Caleb's out there to escape being outnumbered. There's just him and Spence against all of us. But he looks a little lonely, don't you think?"

Lonely? That wouldn't be the word Lauren would have used to describe the handsome man hunkered down on the top step. The peace she'd felt with him early this morning had stayed all day. It had stuck in her heart like a piece of the hushed Montana morning. No, she would describe him not as lonely but invincible. That's how he looked silhouetted by the sunlight, as rugged as the Rockies dominating the horizon behind him.

Aubrey plucked the beaters from the open drawer. "He hasn't dated anyone that I know of since he came back from Seattle. No one special, anyway. How about you, Lauren? Are you dating anyone special?"

Why did she have a feeling that her sister's

question wasn't entirely innocent? "I'm not really looking to date."

"Sure. I understand." Aubrey plugged the beaters into place. "It's tough to meet the right guy, isn't it?"

Still seated cross-legged on the counter, Ava rolled her eyes. "Here it comes. Brace yourself, Lauren."

Brace herself for what? Lauren glanced around, looking to the other women around the room—her sisters. Rebecca was shaking her head in mild disapproval, stirring gravy at the stove.

"What?" Aubrey asked them innocently. "I was just making conversation. Getting to know more about our baby sister."

"You're trying to find someone for poor lonely Caleb." Ava didn't bother to hide her amused grin. "Hel-*lo?* You can't fool me."

"Well, I guess I didn't mean it like that. I was just saying that he's lonely and Lauren isn't dating anyone special. So, why shouldn't they be friends?"

Lauren thought about Caleb this morning and a cozy curl of happiness wrapped around her heart. Friends would be nice.

"Besides, we all know how hard it is to find the right man." There was no mistaking Aubrey's happiness as she reached for the butter dish.

"There are a lot of Mr. Yucks out there," Ava agreed. "I know. I've dated most of 'em."

That seemed to make everyone laugh. Actually, she pretty much agreed with Ava. Her past had been filled with Mr. Yucks, thanks to her mother. And during her grade school years, even Lauren figured out how trusting the wrong men—and every one of them was wrong—could lead to heartache and devastation.

"I'm just saying," Aubrey said over everyone's good-natured comments. "I got lucky with William. Ava, Fate took favor on you with Brice—"

"And probably a little pity," Rebecca winked.

"Probably!" Ava agreed. "Lauren, William proposed to Aubrey at Katherine's wedding reception right here in Gran's backyard. Talk about romantic. She didn't suspect a thing. He kneeled down to pop the question in front of all of us. It was super."

"It was," Aubrey chimed in happily.

"What about me?" Rebecca piped in from the stove. "I know you guys don't like Chris, but he really does love me. And it just proves that Aubrey's right. It's extremely hard to find the right guy. You've got to have the same values and you need to have lots of things in common. And, right there, how hard is that to find?"

The lightness faded from the room. Apparently the sisters didn't quite agree. Aubrey abandoned the mixer and crossed the few yards to the stove. She put her hand on Rebecca's shoulder and gave her a sisterly hug.

"Rebecca, you are worth so much to us. Remember that. The right man will love you even more than we do."

"Oh, he does," Rebecca insisted.

Lauren's stomach cinched up. See, this was the silver lining in growing up the way she had. She couldn't be easily fooled by some guy. She'd watched it happen to her mom. Rebecca had grown up with Dorrie, who was obviously the most wonderful mom ever, and with older sisters and Spence looking out for her.

All of them, she realized, had a faith in relationships that she didn't understand.

"As for Caleb," Aubrey continued as she sliced fresh cucumbers from the garden. "He was engaged a few years back, but it didn't work out. He's been alone ever since."

Lauren winced. How many times had she heard that now?

Ava picked up where her twin left off. "Plus, Caleb has a serious *wow* factor. He is a definite Mr. Wishable. So you really should go out and help him, Lauren. Really. Even I think he's a really good guy and I used to be really skeptical."

She could see what was going on here. "If he's so great, did any of you ever date him?"

"Not my type," Ava offered.

"Not mine either," Aubrey agreed.

"He's like a cousin or something to me," Rebecca chimed in. "I've known him forever. Besides, I have Chris."

"We know you do." Ava shook her head, but not unkindly. "I'm keeping my mouth shut, Becca, don't worry, but you know how hard that is for me. I'm really trying."

"I know you are." Rebecca seemed indulgent as she lifted a frying pan off of a burner and onto a trivet. "Lauren, if you go outside and help Caleb, it should be because you want to help him. That's a lot of corn for one person to husk. Not because our two engaged sisters have romantic stars in their eyes. I'm on your side."

"Thanks. I've never had sisterly solidarity before. It's nice. That is a lot of corn, so I'll just go out to help him. But that's the only reason."

"Great." Aubrey turned off the beaters to add a touch more milk. "Take another paper bag with you. It's right there by the door. Caleb will probably need it."

Snagging the folded up grocery bag on the way out, Lauren forced her feet to take her out the door. She wasn't eager to see how he was doing. Really.

Caleb didn't look up at the sound of the door closing behind her or at the pad of her flip-flops on the porch boards. He grabbed another ear from the pile and began to part the silks. "I wondered how long it would be before they sent you out here."

Lauren glanced over her shoulder through

the window and sure enough, all three sisters had stopped work to watch them. "Could you hear what they were saying or something?"

"No. But I've known the lot of them most of my life. I know what to expect from those McKaslin girls, so don't let it worry you. Pull up a step and sit for a spell."

She took the step below him. "It looks like you could use a little help."

"I wouldn't say no. Spence went off to take a look at Mary's pool pump and that's why I'm alone here with all this corn." He swiped the stray silks from the bright yellow kernels of the newly husked cob and added it to the pile in the plastic dishpan. "Are those girls still watching us?"

"Yes."

"Don't let 'em embarrass you. They mean well." Caleb added the ear to the almost-full dishpan. "I suppose they mentioned my failed engagement."

"It was mentioned." Lauren reached for a corncob and began husking it efficiently.

He reached for a new cob. "Is that a sympathetic look on your pretty face? Or am I imagining it?"

"It's painful when a relationship doesn't work out, whoever is at fault."

"You just leaped to that conclusion, did you?" He tried to keep his tone light; it must have worked because she smiled. This was enough to cover up the sense of regret that had always hung on to him. He yanked at the stubborn green husks. "You're wondering why it didn't work out, but you don't want to ask me."

"Maybe. I don't want to bring up anything painful for you."

"But you're curious. I can see it."

"Well, sure. According to my sisters, you're the best catch around."

That was a good one, he thought, choking on a laugh. "They were trying to show my good points first, before they told you what happened. Or, they wanted me to do it, because it would probably sound more sympathetic."

"Why, what happened?"

"Remember when I told you I lived in Seattle?" He kept working, mostly because it gave him somewhere else to look instead of into those compassionate violet-blue eyes of hers. He didn't want any more reasons to like her, and if she was any nicer to him, that was gonna happen. "You notice how I'm not living there now?"

"You didn't like living in a city?"

"It wasn't so bad. There was a lot to like about it. I served on the Seattle PD for four years. I was doing all right for myself. Lived in a good part of the city. Met and proposed to a real nice lady. Then Grandfather fell ill. It was terminal. I came home to help out."

"And your fiancée didn't come with you?"

"She said that my going home to help out was one thing. Moving there was another. After Grandfather passed, my grandmother had fallen ill and nothing was going to make me leave her alone. Jayna had been born and raised in the heart of the city and didn't want to leave."

"I'm sorry."

"Me, too. At least I knew where she stood before we'd walked down the aisle. I'll always wish that she had the same values." He didn't look up but reached for another corncob. His sadness seemed to fill the air. "What about you? Did you leave any broken hearts behind in California?"

"Me? Not even close. I don't date, because I don't think I can marry anyone." Lauren inspected the yellow cob, pronounced it silk-free and set it carefully onto the towering pyramid of corn. "I don't think I can trust anyone that much."

"Trust? I guess I've never thought about it that way before."

"When you trust enough to marry, you are placing everything in your spouse's hands." Lauren went to work on a final corncob. "When you're married, you're affected by that other person's decisions and actions in every single facet of your life. Your money, your happiness and welfare, how you live, where you live, how many kids and how will they be raised, and you can even be legally affected."

"You're right, hands down." He watched her intently, as if he were trying to figure her out. "That's a pretty extreme view for a pretty young lady to take. You didn't have a relationship go bad?"

"No. I've never let anyone get that close to me. I've never been able to believe that there's a man out there who could be good and kind and faithful and not hurt me in any way. My mom…living with her was lesson enough."

"That's too bad." Sadness—and understanding—marked his face, and he looked away, as if that were answer enough. "I have a healthy respect for marriage. Most of my friends are husbands and fathers. It's a big job to commit to, provide for and cherish a wife. When I take that step, I want to make sure it's right. I see it as a promise. I never much thought about the trust it would take."

"A lot. More than I have."

"But that's what marriage is all about."

How could he imply that it was no big deal? Probably because he had much different experiences in life than she'd had. "You don't seem terrified by that, but I am." She gave the cob in her hands one last swipe to dust off the stubborn silks and slipped it into the full dishpan. "There. Done."

His hand caught hers before she could pull away. His thick, stronger fingers covered hers in a firm grasp, but not an imprisoning one. She *could* pull away if she wanted to, she just wasn't sure if she wanted to. His touch felt as solid as the stalwart man.

No, she'd never met a man like Caleb before. He'd given up his life and risked a relationship just to care for his ailing grandparents. That kind of care took sacrifice, and she respected him for it.

"I take a more optimistic view of things." Caleb let her go.

She withdrew her hand although her skin tingled from nothing more than his touch. "Are you saying I'm pessimistic?"

"Oh, no. It's a free country. Everyone's got the right to their opinions. The thing is, that sometimes people surprise you."

"You're a cop and you say this?"

"Hey, I see the worst side of humanity, hands down. Absolutely. But I've seen the best side, too."

"The best side?"

"Sure. People stopping to help find a missing child or joining a search for an Alzheimer's patient who'd wandered off from home. Every day, I see a lot of good people who care about others. Not just the harm done, but the goodness."

"What do you mean?" He intrigued her, she couldn't deny it.

"Have you met your stepsister Danielle yet? No? Well, her husband's a state trooper who was shot in the line of duty. You never saw such an outpouring of prayer and casseroles and generosity. Folks who'd never met him donated money and time, held car washes and other fundraisers across the county. That's just one example."

"Sure, people can be charitable."

This was an argument he wasn't gonna win, Caleb could see it. But that was okay. Like he'd said, everyone had a right to their take on things. He wondered about Lauren's life. It didn't look as though she got the best end of things, growing up with the parent who couldn't handle responsibility. And he had to agree when he looked at her side. "It can get tricky. People letting you down, why, that takes on a private hurt in a way that nothing else can."

She didn't say anything as she tidied up the work area from fallen bits of husk and silk. He got to his feet and hefted the loaded dishpan. They were done with the husking, but he wasn't ready for this moment between them to end.

The fall of early evening light seemed to gild her and frame her with a rich, sepia glow. She was timelessly lovely. He wanted to tell himself not to notice, but it was too late for that. He was already captivated by the goodness he saw shining through her at that moment.

A smarter man would look away.

He wasn't a smart man, apparently. He was in serious danger of going from neutral-liking her to serious-liking her. Wasn't that something to avoid?

He broke away, heading toward the kitchen door.

"Caleb?"

He ought to keep going, but he stopped. If he looked at her his heart would tangle right up, wanting something he couldn't have, not with this woman, anyhow. She was dead set against marriage and he was ready. Finding the right woman was the problem. So he waited, his back turned to her.

"You were right. Everything turned out well with meeting my family. Thank you."

"Not a problem."

"Are you staying tonight?"

"No, it's your homecoming supper." The invincible line of his shoulders tensed. "I just stopped by to help out Mary, is all. I'll just set these inside and be on my way."

"That doesn't seem right. I—"

"I'll be over tomorrow night for your nephew's fifth birthday party. And there's always tomorrow morning, if you're up to it." He nodded once in the direction. "There's your dad now. I'll leave you two alone."

Dad? Her entire being froze at that word. She turned toward the driveway at the gray SUV pulling to a stop. If she hadn't been sitting, her legs would have failed her. She gripped the lip of the step and held on, her heart lifting at the sight of her dad.

Sunlight glinted on the windshield as the driver's door swung open. She saw an older image of the man she'd studied in the family photographs. She recognized the hawk-like nose and the square jaw, that dependable look. This was the man she feared hadn't wanted her. But there was no chance of that. She knew it in an instant.

"Lauren. Well, now. Howdy. It's good to see you here." He held out his arms, eyes glistening behind his glasses. "Come give your old dad a hug."

"Hi, Dad." She shot off the step. Her bones felt like water and her knees like rubber, but she made it into his arms, felt her Dad's love for her as he gave her a sweet, fatherly hug. She held on with all her might. She had a lot of questions, but the answers didn't really matter. Her father wanted her. That was all she needed.

Chapter Seven

Caleb climbed out of his truck and into the soft golden-rose hush of the morning. Was it his fault that Lauren was on his mind? He'd done everything he could to distract himself from thoughts of her, but still he wondered how her evening was. Crossword puzzles, prime-time news shows and reading. The most those things had done was temporarily distract him. He couldn't explain why he was powerfully interested in her. Just like he didn't know what to do about it.

Part of the problem was his conscience. He'd agreed to Spence's request but didn't feel comfortable with it. He'd called a friend who owed him a favor, a private investigator. He'd meant to help a lifelong friend, but instead, he'd promised to invade Lauren's privacy. There was nothing—not so much as an unpaid parking ticket—in her past. She was squeaky clean and paid her bills on time. It troubled him that he had done this, but he had a bigger problem. The truth was simple: He'd never looked forward to his morning ride this much.

He spread the grain out, keeping one eye on the north-facing side of the carriage house. He could just see it through the tangle of the flower garden. All seemed quiet. The horses shoved, trying to get the most grain, but did he notice? Not really.

Lauren. He'd seen past her words. Past the tidbits about her mother. About her childhood. About not being able to trust people. She'd been let down in life, but she didn't strike him as being beaten by it.

"Hey, cowboy."

The bucket slipped from his fingertips and clattered on the truck bed. There she was, wading through the knee-high grass in worn jeans and a UCLA T-shirt. His senses were attuned to the pad of her shoes against the path, the whisper of her movements, the shy way she smiled at him. Her heart-shaped face was shaded by his gray Stetson. It looked good on her, the light color complementing her golden hair, her violet-blue eyes and her peaches-and-cream complexion.

It made her look like the Montana girl he'd always hoped he could find.

The trouble was, she wasn't a Montana girl.

She held up a small brown sack she was carrying. "How about a barter? A riding lesson for a chocolate muffin?"

"Is it one of Ava's? She's the best baker in the county, you know."

"It's one of her chocolate chocolate-chip muffins. It sounds like way too much sugar, but I bet it's the best muffin in the entire state."

"You've got that right. Ava's bakery has a discount for police- and firemen. She has a rush every morning. We stand in long lines for these." He hauled the bridles out of the storage box and tried to act like he wasn't seriously glad to see her. Not an easy thing to do. "You have a good family dinner?"

"It was very nice. Normal. Spence refuses to talk to me, but that's okay. Other than that, we had a barbecued dinner with all that fresh corn, which was wonderful. We sat around looking through photo albums that Dorrie was thoughtful enough to bring so I could see the years I missed. There were even pictures from before Mom took off with me that she'd found and put into an album."

"Did it help you with your missing memories?"

"No. But it's the present that matters and everyone was so kind. And funny. I laughed until my sides hurt."

With that joy sparkling through her, he was starting to get the notion that he could really like her. He cleared his throat. "Did Danielle come?"

"No, but I'll meet her and her kids tonight." Lauren turned back to gaze thoughtfully at Mary's house. Last night, she'd been part of the family, but she still felt like an outsider. Everyone tried to include her, but she'd never realized exactly how much history and love could tie people together. She didn't have those ties with them. She hoped one day that she would.

"How did things go meeting your dad?"

She thought of the father who'd impressed her so much. "He was convinced I didn't want to know him. He's been sending money to help with my school, even though he's no longer responsible for child support, of course. But he was sending it to my mom."

"That doesn't put your mom in a good light."

"No, but some people are like that. It's sad, but true."

"It's gotta be a relief to know what really happened."

"It makes all the difference. I thought I was all alone but I'm not. I have this extended family who have just swept me into their circle." She didn't know how to say what she meant. Besides, it was too personal.

Caleb had lowered the tailgate and was reaching for a thermos. "I guess this means you'll be coming home for the holidays. Vacations. That kind of thing."

Was it her imagination or did he seem glad about that? Well, maybe she was, too. "Beyond all doubt."

"Then I guess I'll be seeing more of you. Too bad."

The way he said it, with a wink and a grin, made Lauren wonder if he was looking forward to being with her. Who was she kidding? She was starting to really like him.

"It *is* too bad," she quipped. "I'll just have to suffer. That's how much I want to go on another horse ride."

"I figured as much." He gave her his lopsided smile with just one dimple. "Good thing my teaching you to ride isn't a time-limited offer."

Plus, Caleb has a serious wow factor. He is a definite Mr. Wishable. Why was she remembering Ava's words?

Maybe because she was in total agreement. The trouble was that Caleb wasn't her Mr. Wishable. But there was nothing wrong with being friends. It might be a unique experience for her.

The horses had finished devouring their oats and had lined up along the fence, heads up to sniff the wind, gazes glued to the little treat bag she carried.

Caleb patted the tailgate. "Hop up. I brought tea for two."

Nice. She eased onto the tailgate, letting her feet swing in the seed-tufted grasses and unwrapped the sack.

When he handed over the steaming cup he'd poured for her, their fingers brushed. A jolt of emotion zinged through her like lightning out of a clear blue sky. Hot tea sloshed over the rim and onto her fingers. What was that about?

It was just wishful thinking, she realized. How could she not like him? He was a ten out of ten. It was in his manner, the steadiness of him and the easygoing way he accepted people with trust and faith. Especially her.

Yup, he was a definite wow. She was glad she'd taken the risk of opening up to him instead of pushing him away.

Caleb handed her one paper-wrapped muffin. She'd never seen anything so cute. The enormous muffins had monster faces decorated across the top with colorful icing.

How fun. It put a smile on her face and she felt lighthearted as she took a bite.

Delicious. Major sugar rush ahead, Lauren thought, but what a nice addition to an already perfect morning.

Caleb hopped from the tailgate with a two-footed thud. "Are you up for a new challenge?"

"It's the right morning for it, don't you think?"

"Then don't say I didn't warn ya. C'mon, city girl, I'll teach you how to trot. You'll like it. Eventually."

It was the sparkle in his eye that caught her and she found herself following him. Thinking about the man and not the horses. Caleb made it even harder as he cozied up to his gelding, talking low to him.

Wow. She really had to stop using that word to describe the man. What else would fit? Awesome. Inspiring. Perfect. He rubbed Leo's nose and it was hard not to admire the man's quiet command.

She had grit, he had to give her that. Caleb pulled Leo to a stop and when he saw Lauren fall slid to the ground to offer her a hand up.

There was that shot of emotion again, straight to his heart. Her hand was small tucked in his own and her fingers were slim and long, like an artist's. He tried to act as if he hadn't been affected as he pulled her to her feet.

"You okay?" he asked. So he cared. It wasn't a crime, right?

She nodded but not even her first fall had seemed to dim her enthusiasm. "That was kind of fun. Except I don't think I like trotting."

"No one does. But you've got to master it if you want to gallop."

"I'm definitely up for the sacrifice. I'm having the best time, Caleb."

"I can see that. You're beaming." Instead of moving away, he leaned closer. "Wait. You have a streak of dirt on your cheek."

Breathless, she waited while he leaned closer still. The brush of his thumb across her sun-warmed face came as softly as a promise kept. He towered over her, so near she could smell the rain-fresh scent of the fabric softener he'd used on his T-shirt, see the thrum of his heartbeat in the base of his throat and hear the rasp of his step as he backed away.

"Let's get you on that horse—" he gathered Tasha's reins "—the morning is slipping away."

Already the sun was completely above the mountains. He was right. He'd have to leave for work soon and she had a full day planned with family. Family. Her heart punched with the word. Wasn't that a change for the better?

Careful, Lauren. Be careful. Your hopes are getting way too high.

Her experience with high hopes was that eventually they'd pop like a too-full balloon and then where would she be? She'd be home, in her tiny apartment near campus, that's where. Caleb knew it, too. She could visit here, but this was not her life.

And it could have been, she thought with regret. The ghost of a memory whispered, but she couldn't see it. She couldn't make out the voice or the words.

"Lauren? Are you hurt? You fell pretty hard."

She shook her head clear, not sure if she was disoriented by the hint of an almost-memory or by Caleb's caring. His hand settled on her shoulder, bridging more than the distance between them.

"I'm fine. Just thinking about the past, is all." She shrugged away the last vestiges of the memory and let him give her a boost onto Tasha's back.

He kept a protective hold on her ankle. "Just want to make sure you keep your seat. You hit that ground hard."

She meant to tell him that she wasn't rattled, but realization hit her harder than the ground had. She was rattled, but not by the fall.

By him.

It was easy to see the care that he took with her. If only she'd grown up here. If only she could be the kind of girl who could believe in happy endings and real love. If she could trust people the way he could, then so much of her life would be different. Would it be like this?

Maybe. But the truth was, the past couldn't be changed. She could not be the girl who had that much belief in people. So she took over the reins, straightened her spine and accepted the gray hat he'd rescued from the ground.

"I'm going to keep at this until I master it," she told him. "Any more suggestions?"

"Saddling up is too much trouble during the week, but come this weekend, how about I saddle the horses up. You'll be here come Saturday?"

"Yes." How could she have forgotten? The days were ticking by already. She had to savor her time here, this friendship. And if she wanted to get reasonably better at riding, she had to do it now.

Was it her imagination or did the ground seem even farther away? And she knew exactly how hard it was. She still ached from it. Caleb mounted up and brought Leo alongside Tasha and she didn't notice her hurting muscles quite so much.

"Ready, city girl?"

"I'm ready, cowboy." She pressed Tasha into a walk then straight into a bumpy trot. Her teeth rattled, her vertebrae knocked together. A jackhammer was smoother than this.

"C'mon, stick with it," Caleb encouraged.

She bounced a little to the left, then to the

right and started to slide toward the ground. She muscled herself back into place.

"That's it!" Caleb called out.

Suddenly the hard jarring stopped and melted into pure motion. Tasha was galloping and the smooth roll of it was like flying low over the field. Not even sailing was this fun! Laughing out loud, she held on tight to the mare's mane as they glided together on endless waves of green grass. She savored the sensation, the rhythmic beat of Tasha's hooves on the ground, the whistle of the wind in her ears and the sting as the coarse ends of Tasha's mane whipped her in the face. The ground blurred beneath her as Tasha stretched out and they went even faster.

Maybe too fast. She slipped a little to the left. She gripped with all her strength, from fingers to toes, gritted her teeth and held on.

"That's it!" Caleb called out. "Hold tight! She's gonna hit a trot when she slows. Be ready for it."

The end of the pasture was coming up. The white fence flashed ahead. Lauren could feel the change in Tasha's muscles and she tried to brace herself. But did it work? No, because there wasn't a whole lot to hold on to. The horse slowed, she lost her center of balance. The awful jolting started again, rattling her to the bone marrow, tossing her straight up and straight down.

Oh no, she was slipping. Lauren clung more tightly to the horse but she kept sliding right. She tried to correct and slid left.

"Don't worry." Caleb's shadow fell across her. His hand banded her elbow, holding her up, keeping her from falling. "I got ya."

His presence was a balm to her spirit. His grip was rock-solid. He held her steady and safe, so why did she feel as if she were still falling?

Too much sugar for breakfast, that's what. Lauren righted herself on Tasha's broad back. "Thanks. I appreciate the rescue."

"Anytime."

Down deep, a little part of her sighed. Get a grip, Lauren, and not just on the horse. She was definitely going overboard when it came to Caleb. If she wasn't careful, she was going to be president of his fan club.

She straightened up and he released her. "Why aren't you married? I know you had a bad breakup. But a guy like you, one who isn't afraid of commitment, I don't get it."

"There's nothing to get. It might come as a shock to you—brace yourself—but I'm not that attractive of a guy. Women aren't flocking around hoping I'll propose to them."

"I don't believe that. You don't have a hard time finding dates."

"You've met me, right?" He chuckled and it was endearing that he was honestly humble.

Again, not the kind of trait in a man she was used to.

"Do you see any flocks of women around?" He shook his head. "I'm a little too serious for most women."

"Too serious? I didn't know that was a flaw."

"I work. I have chores. I take care of the horses. My place. Mary's place. Help out my brother and his family when they need it. I don't have a big house. Or an expensive one. Wouldn't want one even if I could afford it."

"Well, then I like serious." If she were the marrying type, she'd be interested. And how scary was that? "I grew up in not the best part of the city. It wasn't east L.A., but it was just

above desperate. I saw too many families torn
apart by substance abuse, abuse, violence, you
name it. Mostly I saw a lot of men who didn't
want to take on the serious part of being an
adult. Well, to be fair, women, too."

"Yeah, I see that part of life, too, in my
work. We don't have a lot of that here. We're
a pretty sheltered town, but we have hardship
and poverty. And I saw my share in Seattle."

"Do you regret your decision to go there?
To leave?" Why she wanted to know that, she
couldn't say. It was too personal of a question
and she didn't do personal, right? At least,
she'd never felt comfortable enough before.
Caleb made her feel safe, even when she was
out of her element.

"Not at all. It was a good experience for
me. As for my broken engagement, it was
meant to be. She wasn't as flexible. Jayna
was—is—a bank vice president. She grew
up along the waterfront near downtown Seattle. Her family belonged to the country club
and had a slip at the most prestigious marina.
That kind of thing. I know what you're thinking. What did a classy woman like that see in
a guy like me?"

"Oh, I think it's pretty obvious."

Caleb hung his head. She said it like a compliment. Like he wasn't such an average Joe and pure country. Well, he was. He wasn't ashamed of it. He'd had to come to terms with who he was when Jayna gave him back the ring. "When my granddad fell ill and Nana couldn't cope on her own with everything, Jayna thought I should hire someone to help out. She didn't get why I objected to that. I wouldn't budge and neither would she. That was that."

He shrugged, as if it were no big deal. Easy come and easy go. But it hadn't been. Not for him. He was the kind of man who loved hard and stuck. "Maybe Jayna's decision makes a whole lot of sense to you, but I've never been able to wrap my mind around it. She just didn't love me enough is the way I see it."

She didn't say anything at first and to Caleb it felt as if she probably thought the way Jayna had. Lauren was used to a faster paced lifestyle, all kinds of choices in amusements and entertainment, shopping and opportunity.

Did she look at him and see less, too? Less

because he was happy starting every day
riding a horse through the long low slants of
dawn's light. Less because he was a man of
simple wants. In jeans and a worn T-shirt and
riding boots, instead of a tailored suit with a
designer label.

She broke the silence between them. "It
doesn't make a lot of sense to me, but then
I've never had a reason to think family was
so important. Not until the last few days."

"Trust me. A good family is worth more
than any riches in this world."

"I never used to understand that. I don't
mean that I didn't agree, just that I couldn't
put myself in those shoes. My mom was
always a painful part of my life. I couldn't
remember my sisters and brother. Or my dad,
although I guess he came down to try to see
me, but I don't remember what happened. I
just thought I wasn't wanted."

"That's a hard way to grow up."

"I saw it often enough all around me. Like
I said, we didn't live in the best part of the
city and there were a lot of broken families
everywhere I looked. Unwanted kids. Broken
women. It made sense. But now, all this—"

"It's a whole new perspective?"

"In one way, no. I worked my way into a better life. I might not be living in a place like this, but I have a clean little apartment in a much safer part of the city, at least safer than where I grew up. It's pretty close to campus. I can see a whole different life and I have been able to for a long time. And coming here makes it real for me. Right now."

"I'm real glad you came." He couldn't deny the connection of understanding that swung like a rope between them.

She took a shaky breath. "I guess I'm trying to say that I think you made the right decision. A good family is one of the greatest things there is. But don't forget that a good man is, too."

"I needed to hear that. Thanks." He tipped his hat to her and tried hard to hold back the tide of regard for her washing right through his heart. And failed.

She tossed him that sweet grin of hers. "I'll race you back, cowboy."

"Don't think I'll let you win, city girl."

But he kept the horses neck and neck, letting her beat him by a smidgeon. He hoped he didn't look as smitten as he felt.

Chapter Eight

In the warm sunny kitchen of Ava's bakery shop, Lauren sat with the twins and sampled another bite of cake. She tried—really tried—to be objective about which type of cake Ava should bake for little Tyler's birthday party tonight. But, truly, what on earth could be better than a triple chocolate cake?

"It's going to be a disaster," Ava predicted from the other side of the large metal work table in the center of the room. She had her hair tied back. Her apron and her T-shirt were streaked with every color of frosting and she seemed totally stressed. "Gran is going to be so disappointed with me. She's going to pull the business loan I talked her into and, voilà, I'll be back to working in the bookstore for a living."

"Hey, I like working in the bookstore for a living," Aubrey pointed out. "And I work here for you for free."

"Yeah, you know I love you for it. I'm just saying, it's like an act of goodwill that I'm not at the bookstore anymore. Haven't you noticed that Spence is in a much better mood because I'm not there?"

"It's an incremental improvement, nothing major. Sadly." Aubrey took a bite of the fudge cake. "I think we should do your peppermint cake. It's different and fun."

"Are you trying to confuse me on purpose?" Ava rolled her eyes. "I finally get it decided between these two and you go and make me doubt everything all over again."

"It doesn't take much," Aubrey teased, leaning closer to Lauren. "Spence really is hard to get to know. He's been like this forever. You shouldn't take it personally."

"I know." Spence hadn't actually spoken to her. It was a little intimidating, but mostly she didn't want to push him. "He looks at me and sees Mom. He thinks I'm like her."

"Just give him time." Aubrey seemed quietly assured; it was easy to have faith in her.

Lauren knew Aubrey was right. "I will. Besides, I'll be gone before you know it, and he'll have all the time he needs to adjust."

A spoon clattered to the tabletop. Ava gaped at her wide-eyed. "You're coming back for Thanksgiving, right?"

"And Christmas," Aubrey chimed in.

"And New Year's. Easter. Birthdays. Oh, and my wedding. It's in April. I think. I keep changing it."

"That's because you're a nut." Aubrey grabbed the fallen spoon and placed it in the huge industrial sink.

"Easy for you to say." Ava went in search of a clean spoon and found it in the third drawer she opened. "You haven't set a date. You just wait and see how hard it is to plan a wedding."

"Maybe I'll wait to learn from your mistakes and then elope." Aubrey's words sparkled with amusement and joy.

Lauren leaned forward and cut another bite

of cake. She'd definitely stepped into an alternate reality, some kind of weird world where everything turned out just peachy. How nice was that? "Is everyone here engaged?"

"A year ago none of us were even dating anyone serious," Ava explained. "Wait. I was dating that chef. Talk about a disaster."

The twins laughed together. Feeling a little on the outside in more ways than one, Lauren watched the sisters share a look. She had no clue what it meant, but Aubrey shook her head and went to the sink to wash her hands.

Ava went back to frosting the cake in front of her. "It's like a family pattern. We go from dating disaster to true love and happily ever after. Katherine did it. I did it. Aubrey did it. Now it's your turn, Lauren."

"No way. You're starting to scare me."

"Nothing's more terrifying than true love. Wait, some things would be. Being on a plane in the middle of engine failure."

"Crow's feet," Aubrey added.

"Mortgage payments. Now that's majorly scary." Ava deftly slathered icing across the top of the square layer cake. "How many dating disasters have you had, Lauren? We need to know if we're going to help you."

"We? Who's we?" Aubrey wanted to know as she reached for the paper towels. "I am not a part of this. Don't answer her, Lauren."

How fun was this? She was absolutely sure she was going to love having sisters. "I'm sorry, but I don't have any dating disasters to report."

"No! I don't believe it." Ava looked astonished. "You don't have any disasters? How lucky are you?"

"Maybe it's just that she wasn't around us for our bad dating luck to rub off on her, huh?" Aubrey suggested.

Lauren already loved these two, hands down. "I don't have any disasters because I don't date."

Aubrey sighed and placed her hand over her heart. "I didn't date, either. Well, until William, and I tried not to date him."

Ava rolled her eyes. "Don't we all try that? But when true love is in a girl's path, she has no choice but to crash headfirst into it. So, tell us about Caleb. We've heard through the grapevine that you've been meeting him early in the morning. You could have mentioned that last night. What's up?"

Didn't she know this was coming? Lauren took a sip of milk to wash down the chocolate. "If I tell you the truth, you won't believe me."

"Try us." The twins said in unison, both leaning on the edge of the table in great anticipation.

"He's teaching me to ride. I've been learning on Tasha."

Ava looked a little disappointed. "You're taking riding lessons from him? That's all? No, that can't be right. It's more than that."

It wasn't hard to see that Ava all too easily believed in love. And why wouldn't she? Evidence of it was all around her. In her family, in her extended family, in Dad and Dorrie's example of marriage. How could they understand? Caleb was only…a friend. "Really, it's *only* about the horse riding. I'm leaving in a few days. How could it be more? Besides, riding horses is awesome. I don't understand why you two don't do it all the time."

Ava tsked. Aubrey gently shook her head

from side to side. Apparently, neither of them believed her.

Ava spread the last uncovered spot on the cake. "It sounds like denial to me."

"Oh, you." Aubrey disagreed with a cheerful grin. "Not everyone goes through denying things like you do. Okay, quick change of subject. Only one thing comes close in importance to romance and that's horses. I'm with you, Lauren. If I didn't have to make a living, I'd spend all day, every day, riding my Annie."

"You have a horse?"

"She's not just a horse but my best friend. Do you want to meet her? I've got time, as soon as I finish Tyler's birthday shopping. I have one more thing to get."

"I need to shop, too. I don't have anything for him."

"Okeydoke. We can go shopping together. This will be so fun."

Ava tossed the spatula into the sink. "Hey, we haven't finished talking about Caleb. We need to tell Lauren his finer selling points."

Lauren filled up with happiness. It was a

cozy feeling being with them. "I don't need a list of his finer points."

"You mean like drop-dead gorgeous?" Aubrey asked.

"Totally together and dependable?" Ava added.

"Kind and trustworthy?" Lauren winced. Had she really said that?

"Ha! I knew it." Ava grabbed a rolling pin. "Lauren's sweet on Caleb."

"Well, of course she is." Aubrey cut more slices of cake and trayed them. "We've all been a little bit sweet on Caleb."

"He was my first crush," Ava admitted. "I was five. Remember? It was at school. He gave me his cookie at snack time when I dropped mine on the floor. I was hooked. Of course, he was always hanging out with Spence. So, that was the reason I could never actually fall for him. Too brotherly."

"Yeah, but kind. Trustworthy." Aubrey sighed fondly. "More men should be that way."

Lauren's soul sighed in agreement. He'd said women weren't flocking around him hoping to marry him. He seemed to think he wasn't such a great catch. He was humble. But then he'd taken a hard blow. It hurt when someone you loved loved something else more than you. This was the story of her childhood, over and over again. So she knew a little bit of how deep that could cut at a person. Caleb deserved so much more. He was a fine man. Not for her, sure, but for someone.

Aubrey turned toward the door. "I think I hear the munchkins!"

The pound of little-boy feet echoing in the front room confirmed it. The door swung open and a little boy with brown hair sticking straight up dashed into the kitchen. The birthday boy wore a plastic fireman's hat and a badge on his blue T-shirt. "I got to drive the fire truck an' honk the horn an' see *everything!*"

Okay, she was charmed. Not only by the little boy so cute and excited, but also by Danielle. A pretty, slim woman with dark hair and little Madison on her hip.

"We were invited to the fire station for a birthday visit," Danielle explained as she pulled up a stool. Madison spotted the bright pink fondant on the table and tried to reach for the pretty frosting flower Ava was making. "Hi. You must be Lauren. It's nice to meet you. That's Tyler and this here is Madison."

Lauren hopped up from the stool. A new sister. She liked Danielle immediately. "It's good to meet all of you."

Ava handed over one sugar paste flower to each kid and gave each a smacking kiss on their cheeks. "Okay, out of my kitchen now."

"But Aunt Ava! Can I have a really big, big piece of cake?" Tyler pleaded, one hundred percent charming.

"Sure, kiddo, but only a very tiny, itty-bitty piece."

Lauren took the tray and noticed there wasn't a tiny piece of cake on any of the plates, but there was one huge slice. Probably Tyler's, she figured; the boy gave a war whoop when he spotted it.

"All right!" Cute as could be, he thudded to the door, leading the way into the front. "Guess how many fires I put out today?"

"I don't know," she told him. "But a good

fireman like you probably puts out a lot of fires."

"Yeah. Lotz. Five whole fires. And next we get to go to the water park," he explained as he picked out a table among the dozen or so in the little dining area and pulled out a chair. He climbed on, knee first. "The *water* park," he repeated. "That'd put out *lotza* fires."

She liked her little nephew. She slid the plate with the biggest slice on the table in front of him. "I suppose this is yours."

"Yep!" He gave her a beaming grin.

Danielle started to drag over a baby seat.

"I'll get it," Lauren told her as she set the tray on a vacant table.

"Thanks." Although Danielle seemed to hide it well, up close, she looked exhausted. "I'm sorry Tyler is so wound up. Caleb arranged for him to go to the fire station for a tour, so he wouldn't miss his daddy so much today."

Caleb. There he was again. There was a lot she didn't know about Danielle's situation, but she could also see the love the woman had for her husband and children. She was Dorrie's daughter, so it didn't come as a surprise.

Lauren was happy to drag the wooden high chair to the edge of the table. "What else can I get you? Something to drink?"

"No, getting off my feet will be treat enough, thank you." She slid her daughter into the seat, but the toddler started to protest and struggle. She tried reaching for the cake and gave a squeal of protest when Danielle gently latched her into place.

"Lauren, you and I haven't had a chance to talk yet. I know my mom has been trying so hard for you to like her. Just as she worked so hard to make us a real family after her and John got married. She's probably going to try to mother you, too, and I know you already have a mom. She means well. She's held a place in her heart for you all these years. I don't mean to sound—" Danielle shrugged. "Do you understand what I'm trying to say?"

Did she. A terrible sting swelled up in her throat so she couldn't answer right away. Why wouldn't Danielle assume that Linda had been a real mother? That it was one thing to be a mom with goals and a career to work on, but another entirely to do so with blind ambition. Lauren cleared the emotion from her throat. "I like Dorrie. I've never had a stepmom before, so I'll just put a place in my heart for her, too."

"Thank you." Danielle blinked hard and slid into her chair. "I think it would be wonderful if you sat down and had some cake with us, so I can get to know you better."

"I'd like that." Tenderness welled through her, a steady slow rise of hope and caring. It sort of felt as if, for the first time ever, she'd found a place to belong—just a little.

For Caleb, his work shift hadn't ended soon enough. A bank robbery kept them tied up for a big chunk of the day and that meant he didn't have much time to give Spence the investigator's report. He didn't feel right about it. But he knew Spence needed reassurance. With that, maybe Spence could resolve some of his worries over Lauren.

Once home, and glad to be there, he hauled himself into the shower. Hot water went a long way to easing the tension that had set into his neck muscles. When he was done, he grabbed the phone to order pizza and caught the red blink on his message machine.

Lauren's gentle alto filled the log house's

kitchen. "Hey, Caleb, I hope you know that you're invited to Tyler's birthday party tonight. Gran wanted me to remind you. So I am. See you soon."

Caleb winced. He'd known that earlier in the day, but he was dog tired now and it had slipped his mind. He appreciated the reminder. The beep that ended the message was followed by another. Mary's voice, this time, so warm and cheerful. "You'd best get your boots over here. I won't accept no for an answer, young man. I'm making your favorite for supper. See you at six sharp."

It was eight minutes after, according to the clock on the wall. Looked like he was already in trouble. He pulled on a T-shirt, ran a comb through his hair and grabbed the gift he'd picked up last week. He folded up the report and took it with him. Spence was going to ask for it. Man, he didn't like this, but he also saw Spence's point. Mary was a very well-off woman, a multimillionaire in her own right, and Caleb knew the real concern wasn't Lauren alone, but her mother.

Lauren's words had stuck with him, even through the tough day. *A good family is one of the greatest things there is. But don't forget that a good man is, too.* It meant a lot to him. A little affirmation was good to hear, now and then. Lauren had a compassionate heart and he figured she had her values in the right place. His respect for her just kept growing.

He climbed in his truck and headed down the road, remembering that first day when he and Lauren had chased the escapee horses. He'd liked her then, right off the bat. Now that he'd spent more time with her, he liked her more. He'd gotten enough glimpses to get an inkling of who she was and what she stood for.

As he guided the truck around the final bend in the road, Mary's house came into sight. His pulse began to skip with a deep anticipation. He was looking forward to seeing Lauren again. And, as if the universe was listening, she was the first sight for his tired eyes. She was tying red and blue helium balloons to the porch rail. The bright balloons bobbed in the wind and tugged at their strings. She made him feel as light and cheerful as those balloons.

He pulled the truck out of the way, so he

wouldn't block in all the other vehicles parked in the driveway, tucked the envelope in Spence's truck and headed her way.

Chapter Nine

Lauren pushed away from the porch railing. Caleb was here. Why did that feel like something to celebrate? The rubber squeak of the balloons yanking against their ribbons, the fragrant homemade pizza smell wafting out the open windows and the rustle of the breeze in the trees faded into the background. Caleb strode through the gravel, looking shower-fresh in a blue T-shirt and worn jeans. He was every inch the salt-of-the-earth man she believed him to be.

"Hi, cowboy." She shaded her eyes with her hand to see him more clearly. "We were starting to wonder if you were going to be a no-show. Mary was about to send Spence down to make sure you were all right. Did you get my message?"

"And Mary's. It was a long day, is all, and I'm glad to be here. I smell homemade pizza. My favorite."

"It was the birthday boy's choice. I've never made homemade pizza before, but I imagine out here you don't have delivery."

"One of the local places in town will drive out to the city limits, about a half mile away, and meet you. Why are you looking at me like that?"

"Doesn't it defeat the purpose of home delivery to drive out to get it?"

"Right, but they didn't used to come out at all, so it's a case of taking what we can get." He paused to look her over. "You sure look nice. Judging by the grin on your face, you've had a good day with your sisters."

"I spent most of the day with Aubrey shopping and stopping to see her horse."

"She's got a pretty fancy stable she rides at. Did you like it?"

"I couldn't imagine jumping, the way she

does with Annie. I barely survived the trotting this morning. Anyway, then I helped Gran get ready for the party."

"You two are getting to know one another?"

"More with each day. Your name was mentioned several times."

"Guess that explains why my ears were burning. Nothing bad was said, I hope."

"That you arranged for Tyler to visit the fire station."

"I know the captain." Caleb shrugged one shoulder like it was no big deal. "Besides, Danielle's husband, Jonas, and I are good friends. When he was dating Danielle, he rented one of the houses on my grandparents' property. Our friendship goes way back. What happened to him was a double blow. When you're in law enforcement and an officer goes down, it's like you going down, too. We're all in this together.

"And I'm close enough to his family to see what it has cost them. Danielle's spent the better part of the past two months at his side, day and night, torn apart not knowing if Jonas would live or die. Not knowing if her kids would grow up having their dad. Tyler's missing Jonas and I just want to help out, make the day a little happier. It's what Jonas would want."

"I've noticed you help out around here a lot."

"Well, I have to do something with my time. Might as well do some good."

Did Caleb know how attractive this humble thing was? "Let's see. You have your own place, take care of Gran's horses, you protect and serve the community by day and help out everyone you can on your off-hours."

"Whew, when you say it like that it makes me dog tired. All I can say is I try to keep up with my responsibilities."

Was it her imagination or did he make her dream? He *was* pretty dreamy. "My grandmother has pointed out that you don't let anyone down. That's pretty admirable."

"Well, I've got shortcomings enough, but I've never disappointed anyone on purpose."

Yeah, she'd already figured that out. She followed him into the house, remembering what the twins had said. That all of them had been sweet on Caleb.

She was starting to feel that way, too.

The screen door squeaked open and Gran beamed out at them. "Caleb! You made it. I saw the report on that bank robbery on the noon news. Glad to see that not one of you boys was hurt."

"We're all okay, and thank you for thinking of us." He tipped his hat.

On top of it, he was old-school polite, too. Lauren was starting to notice the list of Caleb's fine attributes was growing longer. If this kept up, she would need a computer to keep track of everything.

"Lauren, I can see our talk about marriage has gotten you thinking in the right direction." Gran radiated delight. "It's nice to see you kids both together."

"My dear grandmother, I cannot believe you said that." Lauren took her by the hand, overcome by this woman's good will for her. "I can see your high hopes."

"Now, I know what I'm talking about. You two just look right together."

Leave it to her kindly grandmother to leap to the wrong conclusion. She looked to Caleb for help, but he just stood there, blushing. Had he guessed that Gran was at least a little bit right? She *was* sweet on Caleb, and she didn't want him to know. She braced her feet and prepared for the worst. "You know, Gran, Caleb and I are just friends?"

"That's how the best romances start. That's how it was when I first met your grandfather. That's how it was when your dad met Dorrie. When Katherine met her fiancé. Oh, I can go on and on."

"I'm sure you can, but we're friends. *Just* friends." It didn't feel like the truth. But what else could they be besides friends? For a moment, Caleb seemed to have a differing opinion, but, no, that was just her imagination.

No one could look more serious as Caleb rubbed his chin. "Lauren's right. We're just pals. So, Mary, don't you go getting any ideas, you hear?"

Mary lifted her chin, all charm and sweetness. "Why, it's a free country. I can get ideas if I want to."

"That may be, but don't you go settin' yourself up for disappointment."

"Disappointment?" She looked at him as if that were impossible.

Yep, he could see right through Mary—she thought that happy endings happened all the time. He knew it was more complicated than that.

"Lauren's too classy to be interested in the likes of me. It's tough on my male ego to say so, but we might as well admit the truth." He winked, to let her know he wasn't affected by it. But this wasn't entirely true. His heart wasn't going in the general direction he'd like it to. "Besides, Mary, you know you've ruined me for other women. No other lady could stand a chance compared to you."

"You're a shameless flatterer and a smooth-talker, too. In my day, nice girls avoided men like you, you rascal." She chided, although she flushed at the compliment.

Caleb laughed at that. "I'm still more rascal than gentleman and don't you forget it. Lauren, don't believe everything this lovely woman has told you about me. With the way she talks, you'd think I'll soon be up for next year's Most Eligible Bachelor nomination."

Lauren arched one brow as if she had great doubts about that possibility.

Why did that sting his male pride, too? He knew the second he first saw her that they weren't in the same league.

"I don't know that I'd nominate you, young man." Caleb heard Mary's heart in her words. Saw her joy in the gentle hand on her grand-daughter's arm, unable to let go—and apparently unable to stop singing his praises. "Maybe you haven't heard, Lauren, Caleb was engaged a few years back and it didn't work out. He's been alone ever since."

"Yes, I've heard that." Lauren struggled to hold back a smile.

Great. If he wasn't embarrassed before, he was now. "Don't you go putting Lauren on the spot. Likely she's not interested in a country boy like me."

"There's no man on earth like a Montana man, born and raised." Mary glimmered with mischief. "Lauren's a smart girl. Surely she noticed that right away. Right, Lauren?"

If she did, Caleb couldn't tell by the way she blithely pressed a kiss to her grandmother's cheek. "Thanks, Gran, but I'm going to plead the Fifth."

Great. Caleb knew he was blushing ear to ear. He could feel his face heat so he grabbed the nearest thing—the screen door—and yanked it open. What he planned to do, he had no idea, but one thing was sure, he needed to get some distance. Was Mary just being her normal, rose-colored-glasses self? Or had she guessed at the truth—that he was a tad bit, and only a tad bit, smitten with the pretty Lauren McKaslin?

Good going, man. That was pretty much the last thing he wanted anyone to know—especially Lauren.

"Caleb, where do you think you're going, to the kitchen?" Mary called him back. "There's not one more thing to do until the pizza needs to come out of the oven. Off to the patio and relax, both of you. Shoo."

He schooled his face, steeled his spine and willed the blush away—not that it was working. Maybe it was best to escape while he could. "I'm taking a detour. I've got a present to deliver."

"Sorry, cowboy, but the gift table is this

way." Lauren backed across the porch, looking beautiful in her simple denim sun dress. She crooked a finger, indicating he ought to follow her along the wraparound porch. "There's no man on earth like a Montana man, huh?"

What was he going to say to that? He waited until they were out of earshot to answer, for Mary was still standing in the doorway, watching them go off together. "What is up with Mary?"

"She had the perfect marriage, so she thinks every marriage is that way. She obviously has few trust issues."

"Obviously." He wondered if Lauren had guessed how he felt about her. "Did Mary embarrass you?"

"Hardly." Lauren didn't seem a bit troubled.

Take notice of that, bud, he told himself, trying to steel his heart. He kept pace with her, their footsteps synchronous. He had some hope the sound might cover up his disappointment. Maybe it was just his pride, but he'd hoped the idea of their being more than friends wouldn't be so easily dismissed.

"Gran's going to have to try harder than that to embarrass me," Lauren went on easily.

"I suppose your outlook has something to do with the anti-marriage sentiment we discussed awhile back."

"I'm not anti-marriage. I've got nothing against the institution in theory, just personally."

"Oh, yeah?" He kept his voice neutral, but the truth was, he felt a little interested in her answer. Walking on dangerous ground was not a habit of his. Why was he doing it now? He waited.

But they rounded the corner of the house and she didn't answer. The gang was gathered in the back patio, hemmed in by the east wing of the house, the garden and the sparkling pool. A big yellow dog paddled his way across the middle of the pool to the shallow end, where Ava slipped into the water to help him out. Her fiancé, Brice, shook his head, as if he couldn't believe his dog had helped himself to Mary's pool. Manning the built-in grill, Spence had turned his back and was deep in discussion with Aubrey's William.

The clan was growing. Everyone was finding love and getting married. He felt a little left out and this wasn't the first time. More and more his friends and family had married and started families of their own. He'd thought he'd be one of them, but it just hadn't happened. It wouldn't if he kept falling for the wrong kind of woman. And if there was anyone wrong for him it would have to be Lauren McKaslin.

"Hey, Caleb." Spence waved him over.

He glanced around for Lauren, but she had already been drawn away by Rebecca and Aubrey.

Be smart about this, cowboy, he told himself. The trouble was, how did he get his heart to listen?

Resigned, he headed Spence's way. There was the matter of the report to get to him. Then he could put it out of his mind.

As the last line of "Happy Birthday to You" was drowned out by a chorus of cheers and advice, Tyler took a gigantic breath, puffed out his cheeks like a chipmunk's and gave a loud and long blow.

In the middle of the table, sandwiched between two sisters, Lauren didn't think she'd ever seen a cuter little boy. Then again, maybe she was biased because she was now his aunt. And focusing on Tyler kept her from thinking about Caleb. Which wasn't proving as easy as she'd expected.

Tyler got all five candles—thanks to Spence who, standing behind him, sent a little puff in the direction of the final candle.

Tyler didn't notice and raised his fists in triumph. "I did it! My wish is gonna come true!"

"See," Aubrey leaned close to say. "Spence isn't such a bad guy. He'll warm up to you. I've been riding him hard about this, don't you worry. We'll wear him all down and you'll see he's a good egg."

"I'll take your word for it." It was hard to believe with the hard, piercing look Spence sent from the other side of the teak patio table. He didn't seem like a good egg but an angry one.

It didn't take a genius to figure out why. According to Aubrey, Spence had been hurt the most when Mom had made the decision to leave. Spence was the oldest. She had gotten to know enough about the family to see that he took his job as big brother seriously. He watched over his younger sisters with all the diligence and commitment of a good, responsible, dedicated man. He'd been protecting them and taking care of them for many years.

But not her. No, he'd aligned her with their mom and her selfish and often flighty ways. How could she blame him for that? He was doing what she thought was rare in this world: protecting his family. What could be more honorable than that?

That might be troubling her, but not as much as something else. Caleb sat at his side, and he hadn't looked in her direction once. Not once. She could hear his baritone rumble *we're just pals.* The thing was, she was confused about her feelings for him. Was he feeling the same way? Was that what he'd meant by the comment? Or was he not interested in her?

Maybe it was a good thing she'd never given men enough credibility, because now that she'd found a trustworthy one, he was occupying a lot of her mental energy.

"I don't know how to convince him," she told Aubrey in a low voice as Dorrie plucked the candles from the giant cake, which had been made in the shape of a fire truck. "He won't talk to me."

"Yes, he is a problem. I'll think of something. He'll come to love you like the rest of us do."

Her throat ached. She couldn't breathe. Aubrey probably had no idea what her kind words meant to someone who'd spent the last three Christmases alone. One thing she vowed to do was to cherish this family.

"Who wants cake?" Ava called out from the head of the table, where she was cutting the cake into rich, fudgy squares. A chorus of answers rang out. "I do!" "Me!" "Aunt Ava, can I have the piece with the frosted dog?"

I'm so glad I risked coming here.

Deeply thankful, Lauren let joy fill her up, wonderful and rare, as she watched this family—her family.

Cute, excited Tyler couldn't sit still in his chair and he basked in the company of those who loved and adored him. Happy and talking to herself, his little sister sat on Danielle's lap. Dad was shining with pride for his family. Dorrie was holding plates for Ava to load with fat slices of cake and Brice, Ava's strapping fiancé, was handing out the plates. Aubrey and William held hands beneath the table. With tears in her eyes, Gran watched from the foot of the table. Happiness was as sweet as the flower garden's rose scent on the breeze. Caleb and Spence, seated together, were talking about investments.

Caleb. Her attention kept coming back to him.

Dad leaned forward over the table to talk to her. "It kills me how many birthdays of yours we've missed."

She didn't want him to know that she'd never had one like this that she could remember.

"The last one we celebrated with you was your second birthday. I think Mary got you a pony. You got to ride it once, I think."

A pony? Her eyes smarted and she looked again at the little boy, so happy and loved. He had a shocking pile of presents on the present table, but that wasn't his greatest treasure.

"Dorrie and I have already talked it over," Dad was saying.

"Yes, we have," Dorrie added as she slipped

a plate of cake in front of Lauren at the table. "I can't bear to think of you in that big city all alone. It's hardly much of a drive at all from Phoenix to L.A."

"It's doable," Dad agreed. "Hope you don't mind we intend to come visit you once we get back home. Say, maybe we can set aside some time next month to come see you, if it doesn't interfere with what you've got going on."

"We don't want to intrude," Dorrie chimed in. "There, now, you need anything else? More soda?"

"No, I'm fine. Thanks, Dorrie. I'll find time whenever you two can come visit."

"Good, cuz Dorrie's got her heart set on it." Dad cleared the emotion from his throat. "Now, I've got to go give the birthday boy his big present."

Her dad and stepmom wanted to see her. They wanted a real relationship with her. Lauren blinked hard. A dream come true.

As she twisted in the chair to get a better look at cute little Tyler, she caught sight of Caleb. Talk about dreams. The man had retreated to the shadows underneath the extensive awning above the long row of sliding doors. He'd crossed his arms over his wide chest. His hair, which had been damp from a shower when he'd shown up, had dried with a slightly tousled look. Was he impressive? Yes.

A Mr. Dreamy? Yes.

A hundred on a scale of ten? Beyond all doubt.

But there was something else that drew her beyond his good looks and fine character. Mary's words circled back into her mind. *There's no man on earth like a Montana man, born and raised.*

Yes, she'd absolutely noticed that. He must have felt her gaze because he turned toward her with those dark, kind eyes of his. She had to fight hard to keep quiet the sweetness filling her heart when she looked at him.

Maybe it wouldn't hurt to start believing in dreams again.

Just friends, she'd said. Well, that wasn't how he was feeling about her, Caleb thought as he watched Lauren rise from her place at the table. He wasn't fooled by Mary's invitation for tonight. This was a family event, and as soon as the presents were done, he was going to head home. But he'd take with him the lovely image of Lauren looking relaxed and serene and happy. He was glad for her, even if they were just friends.

Just friends. The trouble was, he could hear in her intonation that she was sure of that statement. Maybe he'd best take his leave now. He opened the slider door.

"Where do you think you're going?"

He froze. Uh oh. Busted. Trouble in the form of Lauren had caught up to him. He closed the door and supposed he didn't mind so much.

She carried two plates of fudge cake with bright red icing. *We're just friends.* Why was he letting that comment bother him so much? It didn't make a lick of sense why that was eatin' at him. Because her words were a disappointment to him. Because he knew better than to keep walking in dangerous territory but couldn't seem to stop, back up and get to safer ground. Even when every instinct he had was shouting at him to hurry up about it. She seemed utterly unaware of his conflict.

She presented him with the larger piece of

the dessert. "You look like a man who needs a slice of chocolate cake."

"Lucky for me that you noticed that." He took the plate from her.

She stood beside him so she could watch her family as they chattered over the new bike—with training wheels and a helmet— Dad was wheeling into sight.

Tyler gave a shout of glee. "It's the same color as a fire truck!"

Caleb chuckled at the cute little guy. "Nobody bakes a better cake than Ava anywhere on this continent. Thanks for bringing this over."

"No problem. I don't mind. I'm used to it. I'm a waitress full-time at a family-style bistro."

"I would have figured you for something else."

"Really? It's hard work, but I don't mind. It's flexible around my school schedule—"

"Does that mean you work evenings?"

"Every one but Sunday. The best part of my job is that I get these great meals. I hardly ever have to cook."

Caleb took a long serious look at her. The

more he learned about her, the more he respected her. A full-time job. An internship. All on top of being a good student. "That's a lot of hard work."

"Some days it feels like it's all I do, but I don't mind. I don't want to repeat my mom's mistakes. I got a job as soon as I was old enough to work at the diner down the block." She took a moment to pause over a bite of the rich cake. "Being able to afford school has been worth it."

No wonder she was so independent, he realized. She'd never had anyone she could count on. He couldn't explain why he wanted to be the one she could. Another danger sign he chose to ignore, so he watched Tyler instead. The little tyke was ripping open gifts now, his head bent over his task. Wrapping paper was flying right and left.

"That's mine," Lauren said softly. "I hope he likes it. Aubrey thought it was so funny, she started laughing right there in the hardware store and couldn't stop. She said he'd love it, but I'm a little worried."

"The hardware store? What kind of present did you get him?" Then it was obvious as the little guy held up a coiled garden hose and a plastic nozzle.

"My very own fire hose!" Tyler could have been holding the greatest treasure on earth for all his excitement. "I can put out lotz of fires with these!"

"What do you say, Tyler?" Danielle gently reminded him in that kind way of hers.

"Thank you, Aunt Laura."

He might have her name wrong, Lauren thought, but she didn't mind. He'd launched himself over the few yards and was running, arms out, still holding the hose.

At the last moment, Caleb took her plate, so she could kneel down with both hands free to hug him—and try to avoid being bonked by the coiled hose in the process. It was the tenderest feeling she'd ever known, to have this little boy—her nephew, her very own nephew—wrap his arms around her neck and tell her "I love it! I love it! I love it!" He re-leased her so he could dash back and show his mom.

"You scored big with that one. Good job," Caleb praised.

His regard made a cozy curl of emotion

roll through her. The whole family had turned with smiles of approval to her and she felt like one of the crowd.

One of them.

Chapter Ten

Lauren had never had an evening quite like this. And the best part was it wasn't over yet. After the delicious dessert and massive present opening, the men had helped Tyler figure out his bike, although he needed a lot of help to keep his balance. They played with the other toys he'd gotten, especially the new hose and nozzle.

Content, Lauren decided to tackle the heap of dishes stacked on the kitchen counter. As she rinsed and filled the dishwasher's racks, she tried hard to banish the image of Caleb, kneeling down to uncoil Tyler's new hose from its package. The man had it all, she decided. Character, heart and loyalty. He'd make a good husband and father. And that was high praise, coming from her. Was it possible that she was just a little bit more than sweet on Caleb Stone?

"Lauren? Hello?" Danielle was calling to her, crossing the kitchen with her toddler on her hip. "Wow, you are lost in your thoughts. I don't want to interrupt you."

"No, I'm just out in space." Lauren realized she'd left the water running and turned it off.

"I wanted to thank you for your thoughtful gift. Tyler is in seventh heaven."

"I'm glad he likes it. He's a nice little boy. You look pretty tired. Is there something I can get for you? Some iced tea? Honey and chamomile?"

Danielle paused for a moment, studying her over the curly top of Madison's downy head. "You are so like Katherine. It's too bad you can't meet her. Next time. The three of them—her, her husband and stepdaughter— are in Rome this week, I think. But she'll be home for Thanksgiving. You're coming, right? You're more a part of this family than you think."

It was good to hear. Lauren swallowed hard, trying to keep all those pesky emotions down.

"I understand a little of what you might be going through." Danielle shifted Madison to her other hip. "Spence hated me, too, and when my mom married your dad, I didn't think Spence would ever speak to me again."

Talk about inconceivable. Lauren closed the dishwasher's door. "It's clear he adores you one hundred percent."

"Now. Give him time, that's all he needs. He'll come around. He's not the warm and cuddly type, but he's rock solid and dependable. Now, if we could only find a nice woman to get past that gruff exterior, he might just lighten up and actually be happy for good." Madison began squirming and protesting in Danielle's arms, so she set the toddler down. "There he is, scowling at us through the window. That Spence."

Lauren turned. Yep, there he was in the lawn, on the far side of the porch, talking with Caleb. Her pulse lurched. Why did the sight of that man stop her heart?

She reached for the bottle of dish soap and squirted it into the sink, trying *not* to notice Caleb. The men were apparently packing up all of Tyler's toys and taking them out to the minivan. She felt a tug at the knee of her Capri pants and looked down.

"Bup!" Madison held up both chubby arms, her button face one big smile. Such sweetness.

So she melted completely. "Do you want up, little one?"

"Ha!" Madison knew when she was charming and posed prettily before racing on her pretty pink designer sandals to the screen door. She stretched her little fist as far up as it would reach. "Bup!"

"Sorry, I'm not going to help you escape." Lauren couldn't help but smile adoringly at the pretty little toddler who preened for her.

"She likes you," Danielle commented as she began gathering up the pizza pans that had been left strewn on the top of the stove. "You like kids."

"Sure. I used to babysit a lot when I was

young." It was how she put food on the table, when her mom was between jobs. An ache gathered at the nape of her neck—tension. It was best not to think of those bleak early years.

Madison started jumping up and down. "Bup! Bup! Bup! Bup!" Each word was louder than the last. She kept on going. "Bup! Bup!"

Danielle stacked the last pan and carried the heap to the sink for Lauren, eyeing her daughter. "You are trouble, bubbles."

"Bup?"

Tyler's heavy thump preceded him as he raced along the porch and skidded to a noisy stop outside. He opened the screen door and stepped aside as his little sister toddled out. He patted her on the head like a dog. "You gotta push up." He showed her the secrets of the metal door handle.

Madison went up on her tiptoes, stretched as far as she could reach and couldn't make it. "Bup!"

"Tyler, stop teaching her how to run off." Danielle rolled her eyes. Amusement tempered her words.

"But Mom! I'm the big brother. I gotta show her stuff."

"Kids." Danielle didn't seem to mind too much. "Wait until you have your own and you'll see. I have to stay five steps ahead of both of them. All right you two, to the van. March. Lauren, I just wanted to say thank you again. I hope I'll see you tomorrow, okay?"

"I'd like that."

"Good night." Danielle trailed after her kids, watching over them. The older boy took his baby sister by the hand, guiding her safely along the sun-dappled porch.

There stood Spence in the driveway, visible through the rustling leaves, watching over children and mother. And beside him, Caleb.

His gaze found hers, and the distance between them melted away. That rise of emotion and sweet ribbon of tenderness filled the chambers of her heart. No man, ever, had made her feel like this. No man ever made her vulnerable to the core with one look. She really liked this man.

And he was coming her way. Panic shot through her and she flipped on the faucet. Hot water churned into the sink and she grabbed the folded dish cloth from the neck of the faucet. Had he guessed what she'd been thinking—had it been on her face? Maybe what troubled her most was that she didn't understand what she felt for Caleb. Perhaps it was better left unexamined.

His steps knelled on the porch boards. The screen door squeaked open. As he ambled toward her, he filled the threshold. The door shut with a muted thud. "You in here doing dishes all by your lonesome? You should be out there." He gestured through the window where her family was gathering for their goodbyes.

Outside, Dad was swinging Madison up into a big bear hug while Spence watched over Tyler climbing into his car seat. Madison giggled, safe and happy and cherished. Dorrie gave each grandchild a kiss on the cheek in turn.

She turned off the faucet, her spirit tingling from Caleb's closeness. She dunked a pizza pan into the water and started to scrub. Why wasn't she outside? Maybe she'd go with the easier answer first. "I'll go out when everyone's leaving. I wanted to finish up the last of the dishes so Gran wouldn't have to deal with it."

"Your sisters always do that, with a little help from me—"

"From you?"

"When I'm over that is. Don't look so shocked. I've been known to do more than just dishes. I'm single, remember?"

"That's right, the nonexistent flocks of women." She liked that he smiled a little bashfully when she said that. Cute. "I would think your domestic skills would be a draw to prospective brides."

"Sadly, it must not be enough to overcome my flaws."

"I've only seen two so far, but I might see a third."

"You've been keeping count." Amusement warmed the bronze strands in his brown eyes and he moved closer. "Normally I'd be offended, but I kind of like that you've noticed."

His gaze slid to her mouth.

Yikes. A shiver of fear shot through her. Was he going to kiss her? Her stomach plummeted and right along with it any rational thought. For one foolish millisecond, she wanted him to. She wanted to know what that would be like—sweet and romantic and tender, that was her guess. She wanted those things. With him.

Then her common sense hit her like a cement truck. Her head cleared. Her logic returned. She realized she'd dropped the dish cloth and moved away from Caleb to look for it.

Whew. That was close. She scrubbed really hard at the pizza tray, even though it was nearly clean. He had to notice that she was rattled and, maybe, draw his own conclusions?

She had no experience with this. No knowledge on the best way to handle this. Or to cope. Being sweet on a man was not easy on a girl. Not at all.

He leaned close. Closer. He caught her hand with his. She felt warm soapy dishwater and his comforting touch. His was the kind of singular comfort she needed. This was definitely not easy, she realized, letting go of the dish cloth, but not of him. But it was nice.

"You don't want to miss saying goodbye to everyone."

"No," she agreed, hardly aware of anything going on outside. "I'd better go."

"Say goodbye to your family."

"Yes. Okay."

"I'll finish up in here."

"Sure." She sounded a little flustered as she backed away.

Caleb took a little pride in that. Was he the cause of her nervousness? Sure, it might not mean what he hoped, but at the same time, he wished he'd gone ahead and kissed her. He watched her go with a squeak of the screen door, listened to her gait on the porch deck. It felt like she was dragging his heart after her.

So, he was smitten. He didn't feel the need to deny it anymore. There was nothing wrong with having a tender respect for her, right? It was hard *not* to admire her. She'd raised herself up out of a difficult childhood. She'd done it alone. She was modest and kind and loving, everything he'd dreamed of.

The trouble was, liking her was like running through a minefield. He was in definite danger. He'd been the one to say it. What would a city girl see in a simple Montana man? Maybe he'd have to find that out.

* * *

Throughout the goodbyes to Danielle and her kids and waving them off, Caleb stayed at the front of her mind. Had he thought about kissing her and decided not to? Or had he simply been reaching for the dish cloth?

She was clueless. She had no experience with these things. The possibility of his kissing her scared her a little because, to her surprise, she'd wanted him to kiss her—just for a moment and just until reason kicked in. What was that about?

Out of the corner of her eye, she could see him through the kitchen window, shoulders straight, head bowed as he finished the last few dishes. He didn't look up, but she could feel him watching her. Exactly the way she was watching him.

I'm way too interested in this man. Next thing she knew, she'd go from sweet on him to full-out serious in like with him. Not a smart thing. Especially since they didn't live in the same state.

"Lauren, dear." Dorrie, arms out, wrapped Lauren in a quick hug. "I've got it all arranged. We're going to lunch tomorrow, my treat. All of us girls will be there. We need to make the most of our time here with you. I figure we'll make a little notebook with all our information—birthdays, phone numbers, e-mail addresses, mailing addresses. That way we can stay in close contact with you after you head home. What do you think?"

What a nice lady—and a nice mom. Lauren's heart stung. She would have liked to have known Dorrie—and everyone—so much sooner. "I love the idea. Count me in."

Dorrie brightened. "Wonderful. We'll make it a date, just us girls. And Mary, of course."

"That's right, don't forget me," Gran chuckled from the porch step where she was keeping watch over her family.

Cheerful in sunshine yellow, Ava danced up and wrapped her arms around Dorrie from behind. She sparkled with joyful mischief. "I'm starting to worry, Dorrie. I used to be your favorite, but now it might be Lauren."

"Yes, love, you've been replaced." Gently kidding, Dorrie brushed at Ava's flyaway hair with a motherly hand. "You and Aubrey drive safe. I'll see you both tomorrow."

"Maybe we should invite Spence," Ava

suggested loud enough for her voice to carry across the gravel driveway where their big brother was climbing into his truck. "He needs to spend more time with Lauren, so he can love her, too. Will you come, Spence? C'mon. It'll be super-duper."

Spence tossed Ava a glowering look, did not answer, then slammed the door of his truck.

"I'm just tormenting him," Ava explained, although it was clear she had nothing but love for her older brother—and maybe a little annoyance, too. "Someone has to. He's such a Heathcliff."

Lauren tried really hard not to look back at the kitchen window. "Heathcliff? You mean from *Wuthering Heights?*"

"Yeah, although I've never read the book. Okay, and I haven't seen the old movie. But I get the gist of it, because I grew up with him." As if greatly burdened and not minding it a bit, she shrugged. "Lauren, I'm *so* glad you came back."

"Me, too." The gratitude welled up from her soul. "We have Gran to thank for that."

"Another reason to love her even more, as

if that's possible," Aubrey said from her quiet perch next to Gran.

Dad appeared from the breezeway beside the garage where he'd been tending to bagging up the evening's garbage and recyclables. "Well, I'm beat. Dorrie, you ready to head home?"

"I am." Dorrie sighed, obviously tired, too. "Good night, everyone."

"Good night." Lauren joined everyone in calling out.

Everyone moved away to their vehicles, the twins walking toward Ava's SUV. Rebecca headed toward her compact sedan.

There was only one goodbye left. Distinguished in his summer plaid cotton shirt and jeans, Dad looked like everything a good man should be. After closing Dorrie's car door for her, he ambled through the gravel. He stopped to give Gran a kiss on the cheek and exchange words with her before he headed Lauren's way.

"I'll see you tomorrow, too, right, Lulu?"

Lulu? Was that what he used to call her? She took a step back. She wished she remembered. "I'll make sure to see you. The time is going so fast."

"It is, but that's not a worry. We've got a lot of time. I'll make sure of it. I'm not going to let anyone part us again."

That was a promise she could trust. Her heart squeezed as he walked away.

The rest of the vehicles ambled slowly down the gravel road, their passengers waving out of open windows, calling out their final good-nights. In Ava's case, actually leaning out of the window. Lauren stood rooted in place, watching her family go. Long after the cars had vanished from her sight, the warmth of their affection remained.

When she turned, ready to get back to the dishes, there was Gran smiling at her and loving her and holding out one hand. And, in the window beyond, Caleb watching her with dark, unreadable eyes.

Caleb dried the last of the pizza pans. He hadn't taken his gaze from the window, where he had a perfect view of Lauren. How he was going to stop caring for her, he didn't know. It might appear as if she belonged here with her family, but she had a life somewhere far away. And, maybe, more in mind for her future.

One thing was for sure. If he followed these rising feelings he would be putting his heart at risk. He wasn't a man who liked to get hurt. His gut was telling him, too risky. Move back. Take cover. But his feelings, his heart, well, they weren't obeying.

Watching her in the lengthening shadows of the sweet summer evening made all sorts of protective, caretaking emotions rise up. She was kind and loving and warm, and she drew him. It would be so easy to fall in love with her. Just a few more steps to take, that was all, and he'd be one hundred percent devoted to her.

There was another problem, too. She was a woman who had been very plain about her beliefs. She didn't think she could trust a man with her life and with her heart enough to marry.

Now, a smart man would see that as reason enough to take off out the back door, head home and put every thought of Lauren McKaslin out of his mind.

So, why wasn't he doing it? He hung up

the dish towel with a sigh. He didn't have an answer to that.

He did turn toward the soft sound of her steps. His heart filled with joy at the sight of her. He watched the way she smiled when she found him, and there was no hiding the flash of joy on her face, in her spirit, in the air between them, when she spotted him. It was a joy that matched his.

He gathered his courage and held out his hand. "Come walk with me."

Chapter Eleven

After leaving Gran to rest on the porch swing, Lauren agreed to his request. And once they'd headed down the road and rounded the bend, out of Gran's sight, Caleb moved closer to her. Well, maybe that was her wishful thinking. It was hard to tell for it was a subtle move.

They walked in companionable silence, which was a nice experience. She had to admit she was starting to believe in dreams. After all, this place was real. The Montana beauty really did invite a girl to dream, just a little. How could she help it? The air was scented with ripening grasses and the drifting scent of flowers full-faced in the fields. Larks trilled and the horses lifted their heads from their grazing to nicker hellos. She breathed in the country goodness and peace settled deep into her soul.

Caleb nodded once toward the fence and changed his direction. "Leo's coming over to say howdy."

So they headed through the grassy shoulder of the road to the board fence. Grasshoppers startled out of their way. A jackrabbit a few yards away stopped to wiggle his nose, trying to smell if they were friend or foe. He must not have been too worried, because he slowly hopped deeper into the grasses. A hawk circled in a lazy sweep overhead and, in the distance, deer grazed at the edge of a creek.

"This could be a scene from a Western," she said. "All that's missing are the buffalo."

"The neighbor on the other side of my property has a small herd."

She nodded. She should have known. Leaning her forearms against the sun-warmed board fence, the way Caleb did, she waited for Leo to meander over. She was going to miss this. These wide-open spaces grew on a person.

Caleb gazed out at the horses. "I hear you've got a family thing lined up tomorrow."

"I do." He'd been standing finishing up the dishes the whole time, in front of the huge window over the sink, which had been open to the evening breezes. Sound traveled a long way in the country. "What else did you overhear?"

"Now, I didn't mean to. It's quiet here. A small sound makes a big impression."

"I've never been in such a quiet place. There's no traffic sounds. No airplanes overhead. There's no neighbor noise, no blaring TVs, car alarms, voices, kids playing basketball. Nothing."

"Well, your grandmother owns a few hundred acres. It puts distance between neighbors."

She felt different from the woman she'd been when she'd first driven up this road. Then she was pretty sure who she was, but now? Not so much. Coming here had turned everything upside down. It was like one of those snow globes, she had upended her life and given it a good shake to get the snow to start swirling. Eventually it would calm and every last piece of snow would settle. She took a deep breath and wondered if this was her life settling, finally.

Everything felt different. Better. And this companionship with Caleb was nice. But would the sweetness she felt for him last? She was leaving in a few days. Her life wasn't here.

Yet.

That single word jolted through her brain. Where had it come from? More wishful thinking? Or, in fact, from something more substantial?

"I'll have to pull an early shift tomorrow." He stared ahead at the horses, who had their heads up and were ambling closer. He didn't sound as if it were a big deal to him. "Means I'm on the clock tomorrow by five-thirty."

"Let me guess. You won't be able to take me riding?"

"My regrets. It's a big vacation season and we're short staffed, so I couldn't switch with anyone. Suppose we could make that lesson for another time?"

What he was saying was perfectly logical and reasonable. So why did she feel disappointed? Was it the chance to ride that she would miss, or was it spending time with the man?

Wait. Don't answer that, she ordered to herself. Instead, she took a steady breath and tried to sound as reasonable as Caleb. The calm, logical tone of her voice surprised her. "I understand. I don't think I've told you how much I've appreciated your teaching me. Surely you must have something better to do."

"As a matter of fact, I don't. Besides, I've sort of liked it."

"Me, too."

He didn't look at her, but she could feel his smile. There was no hint of it in his hard-planed face or the stony line of his mouth, but it was there all the same, like a little smile of the heart.

Leo, who'd taken his sweet time walking in the evening heat, nosed up to the fence. Caleb held out his hand to greet his gelding by touch. "Not that I'm much of a rider. It won't take much longer and you'll have to leave me for a more accomplished teacher.

Like Aubrey. Now, she was on the Olympic equestrian team. She could teach you in a way I can't."

"Really? I didn't know that. Although I did get to go to the riding stable where she boards her mare and it's impressive. I guess I shouldn't be surprised."

"I suppose you're interested in the fancy riding. English saddles. Those riding fashions. Jumping."

"I think you have the entirely wrong idea of me." She seemed to think that was pretty amusing. "I'm not so fancy. Haven't you noticed?"

Sound indifferent, man. Hold back your heart. "You seem just fine to me."

"You're not so bad, yourself."

Good to know. He gave Leo's nose a pat. "Maybe when you're back home, you might miss this place."

"There's no maybe about it."

"You have classes starting soon."

"Sadly. I love school, but I wouldn't mind having a little more time here."

"Sure. I get that." He kept rubbing Leo's nose, careful to keep his feelings hidden. It didn't hurt to do a little recon before he took one more step where his heart was telling him to go and his logic was warning him away from. "You must miss home. All your friends. There's a lot to do there."

"At first. I missed it more with every mile that passed on my way here. But Gran has made me feel so welcome and my family makes me feel as if I belong here and—"

"And?" He waited, desperately wanting her to finish that sentence.

"It's been nice getting to do things I've never had a chance to do, like learning to ride."

"I'm glad I could help with that."

She inched closer, just a smidge, so she could stroke Leo's sun-warmed neck. The gelding nickered in approval. "It's been nice getting to know you, too."

"Is that so?"

"Sure. I don't have a lot of time for friends, sad as that sounds. I'm just trying to get through school and improve my life."

"That's an admirable thing."

"You think so?"

"I do." He liked that his opinion mattered

to her. He sure was starting to wonder about her opinion of him. "You work hard. There's nothing wrong with that."

"The thing is, my life isn't balanced. Everyone has family, but I do better when I'm away from my mom." She didn't look at him as she talked, as if that would make it easier to be so frank. "Everything that I was missing in my life was here all along."

"So, it's been life changing?"

"Coming here has changed my whole world. I can see how—maybe—I've kept myself buried in my work and school striving so hard so I don't have to risk getting hurt."

Bingo. She'd said exactly how he'd been feeling for the last few years. "How about that? The city girl and the country boy have this in common."

"You, too?"

"It was the best way to deal with a lot of stuff."

"You've had a lot of loss, too. Your parents, your grandparents, your broken engagement."

"Yep, life has a way of beating all of us with a big stick from time to time. You gotta take the bad with the good."

"That's the hard part about living. My mom couldn't deal with the harder part of life, responsibilities, commitment and consequences. She coped by always looking for the fastest and easiest path out of a problem and that always landed her—us—in more crisis."

"That had to be tough on a little kid."

"Very."

Hold on to your heart, Caleb, he told himself. He tried not to picture her as a little girl with ringlet curls and those big violet eyes and vulnerable the way all children were, the way everyone was—and failed.

It was easy to picture her, all of her, past the protective distance she kept between them. She'd been hurt. He knew what that was like. She was alone. He'd gotten a good taste of it these past few years. Life was a balance of good things and bad things, but it was the choices a person made that determined their mettle. Their character. What they stood for. He could see that in Lauren, too.

Don't fall in love with her, man. But he feared he had already started to fall.

"That's why I've tried so hard," she continued saying. "I saw the mistakes Mom made and where that led her. And I don't want to go down that path, but I think life's taking me there anyway. I hadn't noticed that until now. Until tonight."

"What do you mean? You said you don't want a film career."

"Goodness, no." Lauren couldn't even imagine that; just as she couldn't figure out the right words to say what she meant. Her feelings were jumbled up inside, a big tangled knot. They would take time to sort out. She wanted to escape Caleb, escape being tangled up this way. But how impossible was that? She could run, sure, but emotions had a way of staying with a person.

She took her time, searching for the right words and failing, so she did the best she could. "Mom was so alone. She used to say we were together, we were a team, but that wasn't true. I was a child and there was only so much I could do for her. She hopped from one bad relationship to the next. She was afraid of being alone, but she never let anyone close to her. In a real way, you know what I mean? She's alone now, between marriages, as she's always been. I always prided myself on being different from her. On being more sensible and grounded. On not making the mistake of relying on other people. I guess I thought that was one of her flaws. I learned that you can only rely on yourself. But now—"

She fell silent, and he turned toward her, inching closer. It was not her imagination. Nor was it a trick of the light that made him seem so revealed. He had a big compassionate heart and she adored him.

It was hard not to think *wow*. Hard not to lay her cheek against him. To find out if being held in his arms would offer the safe harbor she wished for. But even thinking about getting that close to him made fear rumble through her middle. She was afraid. But not of him.

She was afraid of finding out if he felt this, too. If anyone looked trustworthy enough for her to fall for, it would be Caleb Stone. And if he did feel the same way, then what? She'd have to actually trust someone on a deep level, which she'd never done before. That meant relying on him. Trusting him. Scary stuff.

Just say it, Lauren. She took a deep breath and took a step on that scary ground. "Now, being here and meeting my family, I can see how intertwined their lives and their affections for one another are. I feel a little part of that, for the first time ever. I have real family ties. And on the other hand, I've never seen myself as so alone."

"What do you mean?"

"This family really cares and it's not superficial. It's deeper than appearance; I've never known anything like this before. I've always been afraid of it. I—" She shrugged.

He leaned closer and picked up where she left off. "If you don't care so much, you can keep yourself safer. You won't be as disappointed or as hurt. Really letting anyone into my heart in a deep way really scares me, too."

"Exactly." Caleb seemed to understand where she was coming from—again. "Exactly. It's how I've lived my life. It's how I'm *living* my life. That makes me just like my mom. Just like her."

"That's not true."

"Isn't it?" He didn't know; he couldn't see it. She thought of her fairly solitary life back home, of the hours she devoted to studying in the graduate library on campus, of the friends she had who were more acquaintances than friends, of the long hours she put in at both of her jobs.

But she had had no lasting relationships. Nothing that mattered. "I think about my mom. How could she have been in this family with Mary for a mother, so devoted and loving, and then married to Dad, so reliable and solid. She looked so happy; there were so many pictures of her smiling. She appeared to be the perfect daughter, the perfect wife and the best mother, but she wasn't happy. What if she always held back her heart, the way I've been doing? Then I'm on the same path, in a way."

She fell silent, holding back one last thought. *I'm afraid of doing that with you.*

The horse was nibbling Caleb's shirtsleeve and collar for attention and not getting any. No, the man's focus was solely on her. He had an intensity like a magnetic pull that drew her a step closer. She longed to open her heart to him. It was a totally new longing, one she'd never had before.

I care about this man. I truly do. The realization frightened her a little more—but it was a good kind of fear. Her grandmother trusted him, her sisters trusted him, why shouldn't she trust him?

Because she'd never trusted anyone that much. It had never seemed like a good idea, to lean on anyone. But everything had turned upside down and she was seeing her life with new eyes. She'd never realized how much in life she was losing out on. In that way she was truly her mother's daughter and it wasn't a legacy she wanted.

"I hold back my heart too much," she admitted.

"It's how you survived a turbulent childhood." The way he said it made it sound so reasonable.

"But at what point does it become taking the easier path? Look at my grandmother. She's lost her parents, her brother, her son in Vietnam, her daughter to disappointment, her sister, her husband and her friends. That's a lot of loss for one woman, but she's the most loving and giving person I've ever known."

"If it's any help, you seem to be doing all right."

"It means a lot to me that you think so." She'd never felt so close to someone. Never felt so vulnerable. Her affection and regard for Caleb grew stronger.

She didn't feel afraid anymore. "This feels like a dream coming true. Being here. Right here."

Tasha had wandered over and Caleb went back to petting the horses, to Leo's relief. Caleb cleared his throat. "The thing about dreams coming true—the real kind—they come around pretty rarely. You gotta grab hold of them or they have a way of passing you by."

She knew he was telling the truth. Her feelings for Caleb had been deepening ever since they'd first met. "What about you?" she asked. "What dreams have you let pass by?"

"I want to show you something." He held out his hand.

There was a silent invitation in his eyes and something indefinable in the evening air between them. Like a dream sailing close enough for her to touch.

So he felt this, too. She placed her hand in his and felt the rough callused heat of his palm when his fingers twined with hers. Serenity rolled through her, greater than any wish, deeper than any hope had ever been.

With her small hand tucked trustingly within his, Caleb did his best to guard his heart. But he feared he was losing it with every step he took down the road and through his property. The sun began to sink toward the mountains, standing low, painting the underbellies of cotton-ball clouds with shades of peach and gold.

He'd never seen a more beautiful evening. Then again, maybe it wasn't the scenery but the lady at his side. Twilight crept around the edges and into the lengthening shadows as he held open his backyard gate with his left hand, so he could keep her hand in his. He didn't want to break the connection between them. He wanted this closeness. Absolutely.

"This is a paradise." Awe softened her gentle alto into a whisper, as if she were afraid to break the silence.

He knew how that felt. He took in the view of the log home, honey-warm, with numerous wide windows reflecting the rosy gold of the impending sunset. The stone fireplaces matched the pathways leading to the front steps and around the house to the generous patio. It wasn't as upscale as Mary's home, but his place could hold its own. Simple native shrubbery were arranged in beds and climbing honeysuckle and roses clung to arbors in the back. The brick grill was new, along with the hot tub. "I made a few improvements."

"I expected a vintage home like Gran's. Or an updated farm house, but this looks like something out of a magazine."

"My grandmother always wanted a log home, so for her sixtieth birthday, my grandfather built her one. It's on the site of the original farmhouse back when this land was homesteaded by Matthias Stone in the 1860s."

"I can't imagine having family roots like this. Until the last few years, I moved about once a year for as long as I can remember. We're standing on the land your great-grandparents lived on."

"And my great-great-grandparents. Pretty amazing, huh?"

"It must make you aware of your place in the world."

"It makes me aware of my family. Of the people who lived well and loved right, who came before me, and my chance here." He guided her along the pathway, underneath the red-rose arbor. "The original rosebush was planted in 1863. When Matthias and his wife's first child was born." Caleb faced the orchard beyond the garden fence. "This is the orchard they planted. The trees have been replaced over time, but it's basically the same as it was in the 1860s."

Lauren took in the sight—the gloss of sunlight on full leaves and ripe fruit, the rustling music of the breeze through the orchard and arbors. There was a mix of old and new. Young, chin-high blue spruce rimmed the boundary between garden and grass and orchard, the patio furniture and hot tub were newly installed, and then there were the roses and hydrangea bushes, ancient and thick with brilliant blooms.

Caleb's hand protectively enclosed over hers *did* feel right. Suddenly, everything fell into place. The realization of who this man was. Of what his family was to him. Of what his life meant here.

"Your grandparents lived and died here," she said. "You took care of them when they were ailing."

"I did, but not alone. My brother and his wife, Wendy, moved back from Denver and put their lives on hold to help out, too."

"You left your life and more behind in Seattle."

"Your life is where your heart is. If the 'more' you're referring to was my fiancée, she wasn't right for me. She wasn't in love with me enough. It wasn't that I wouldn't give up Montana for her, because I would. It's that she didn't get—" He stopped short of saying more.

"She didn't get what family is to you."

"You take care of your family. That is your greatest commitment."

"I never understood that before." She thought of her childhood looking through barred windows and security screens, a childhood of cracked sidewalks to play on and colorful graffiti.

She thought of her mom, always away—

making connections, going to auditions, cocktail waitressing late nights in the worst places trying to make rent money. "My mother always said she was living out her dreams, that she had to be somebody, make her mark in the world. But she had those things here. Love and a committed husband and kids and a childhood growing up here with parents who adored her. I don't understand why she left. I always thought she had nothing here to keep her, but she had *everything*."

"One person's heaven is another's purgatory."

"I suppose, but—" She didn't remember crossing beneath the arbor, but somehow they were in the middle of the yard. She could see colorful hummingbirds suspended in midair as they drank from the honeysuckle trumpets. She thought of Caleb's ancestors who had lived and loved and grown old together on this land. It was so peaceful. "People live great lives every day. It's in how they love and what they stand for when times get tough, staying committed and loving day in and day out, the quiet courage of loving deeply. It's not famous but it is the only greatness."

He studied her for a long heartbeat. The air turned opalescent with the fading light and the landscape stilled. The sun melted into the purple edges of the mountains, draining the light from the sky. The clouds burned like flame.

He broke the stillness. "What are you doing for dinner tomorrow night?"

A trill of hope lifted through her spirit. Was he asking her out? "Nothing."

"How about going out with me?"

"I suppose."

He paused and the sun kept sinking. Her heart waited to beat. When he spoke, his baritone rumbled low, with feeling. With hope. "Do you still think marriage is too risky? That it's trusting someone too much?"

"Not if it's the right someone." She was thankful the sun chose that moment to disappear completely, thickening the shadows and casting their web over her, hiding the affection she knew was on her face. She hoped that Caleb hadn't been able to see.

And hoped that he had.

Chapter Twelve

Throughout the night and all day long, first-date nerves were consuming her. She'd been unable to keep the news from Gran or her sisters. It had been the main topic at lunch, at one of the restaurants near the university campus. It had been fun to share her news and excitement.

However, as evening approached, her excitement turned into a mild case of anxiety. Aubrey had shown up first, for moral support, with Danielle's little ones in tow. Through the front window of the carriage house, they could keep a sharp eye on little Tyler, who was busy with one of the hoses in the small patch of lawn. Madison had plopped down in the middle of the living room and was beating a wooden spoon against a kettle like a drum, making enough racket to drown out the roar of a jet on takeoff.

Aubrey unzipped the garment bag she'd arrived with. "Okay, I raided both mine and Ava's closets and this is the best we have. First, a hand-me-down from Katherine. It's way too classy for either of us, so we've never actually worn it. It's like new. What do you think?"

Lauren's jaw dropped at the little black dress, modest, exquisite and simply cut. The fabric shimmered and shouted, "expensive." "Is that silk?"

"Uh, probably." Aubrey twisted to read the tag. "Yep. You'd look beautiful in this."

"I'll probably spill something on it."

"Okay, I know how that feels. Best not go looking for a disaster, huh?" Aubrey's smile was understanding as she laid the dress over the back of the couch and reached into the garment bag for the next selection. "Here's

Ava's best dress. Brace yourself. It's bright yellow."

As if bracing herself could possible prepare her for the neon flash of that dress. "I've never seen anything that bright and yellow. Not even the sun."

"Okay, enough said." Aubrey set the pretty dress aside and reached for the last dress in the bag. "This is my favorite. What do you think?"

At least it didn't blind her. It was made of soft linen in a lavender shade and had a princess collar. A bias-cut skirt added a little gracefulness. Not too fancy, not too casual. "Perfect. I love it."

"Super-duper." Aubrey beamed as she held the dress up to Lauren's chin. "It complements you. You'll look so beautiful in it that you'll take Caleb's breath away."

"I just don't want him to take one look and run in the opposite direction." Not that she thought that was going to happen, but she didn't know how to say what she meant. She gazed down at the lovely dress. "This is very nice of you, Aubrey."

"Hey, it's what sisters do." Laying the dress

carefully aside, she caught Madison taking off with the wooden spoon toward the open front door, sweeping her up with a kiss to the cheek. "Caught ya! You're not going anywhere, cutie."

Madison squealed with glee. "Bah-bup!"

Aubrey set the toddler back on the living room's braid rug and talked over Madison's cheerful jabbering. "That lavender dress is one lucky dress. Ava wore it to Brice's birthday dinner, right before she got engaged. I wore it the evening that I fell in love with William. So, you never know what will happen tonight with Caleb."

Did she want that? Was it even something she could rationally decide? Her heart seemed to be heading in that direction all on its own. "Let's be cautious. One step at a time. My classes start next week. I have an internship, a job, an apartment, obligations and little time for a long-distance relationship."

"That's not a big deal. You'll make time for one. You'll finish your degree. California isn't that far away. Besides, the campus here has a master's program. Oh, and you've heard of airplanes and cell phones and e-mail, right?"

"Well, yes, but—" She teetered on the edge of hope. How can love prosper with so much distance between anyone? She'd been afraid to let herself think this far.

Last night, walking with Caleb had been so perfect. It should be enough to have a lovely evening sharing meaningful conversation with a worthy man. She was afraid to admit that she longed for more than the life she'd been living. For this kind of life. Maybe with Caleb. And how could she talk about something so personal and new? She wasn't used to having a confidante.

"Thanks for letting me borrow a dress." The nicest clothes she'd brought had been a medium-casual dress that would pack well, nothing as nice as this lavender one. She *did* want to impress Caleb. Was that a bad thing to admit?

I care about him. Very much.

Lauren eased back down on the edge of the couch and carefully packed the rejected dress safely into the garment bag. She noticed that Tyler was tossing down the garden hose and racing toward the little gate, where Ava came into sight. She carried two enormous totes, one over each shoulder.

Aubrey clasped her hands together. "I can't believe it. She's actually on time for once."

"Ava's coming here why…?"

"Sweetie, you have to face the fact that you have sisters now. We are an enmeshed family and proud of it. Believe me, it's easier if you don't fight it. Just accept now and acclimate. Trust me."

"I'm a little afraid to," Lauren quipped. "Enmeshed? Isn't that term used to describe a psychologically dysfunctional family?"

"Sure, but we don't mind. Besides, we like our family that way. You'll come to like it, too, I know it. Hey, when you think about it, Caleb is practically family. He's already used to us, so this could be good if you two fell in love—"

The screen door squeaked open without a knock and in walked Tyler. The little boy dripped water and, as a successful firefighter, walked with great importance, toward the kitchen.

"Whew, it's hot puttin' out fires." He stopped to toss them a dimpled grin, pat his sister on top of her head and then marched to the kitchen where he yanked open the refrigerator door.

"I'm so excited." Ava breezed in, looking just like Aubrey except in head-to-toe pink. "This is totally great. Are you psyched, Lauren?"

"I'm all right." Or trying to be.

Ava rolled her eyes. "It'll be totally fine. You two are like made for each other. Caleb's been majorly bummed for a long time. He needs a soul mate. Besides, you like Montana, right?"

"Sure, but please don't start planning our wedding." She liked that Aubrey started laughing. At least this was going to be fun. "It's only dinner."

"Sure it is." Ava plopped the bags on the floor. "So, I brought hair stuff. And I pilfered Katherine's jewelry, because she has the nicest stuff—"

"Wait, I can't borrow jewelry, too. What if I lose it? I'm worried enough about spilling something on the dress."

"Nope, sorry," Aubrey said, taking one side of Lauren as Ava took the other and sandwiched her on the couch. "This is what we do. So, let's get a good look at you. Ava, should her hair be up or pulled back?"

"Down. I like how she's got a little wave to it. It's bouncy." Ava squinted, in deep thought.

While Madison sang at the top of her lungs and beat the kettle with all her might, Tyler wandered back into the living room with a grape juice box in hand. He headed back outside to fight more imaginary fires and stopped in the doorway. "It's Becca!"

Sure enough, there was Rebecca coming on the walk. Lauren was outnumbered.

"It's too bad Danielle can't be here." Aubrey took one of Ava's totes and unzipped it. "She's still at the hospital. Has she called you yet?"

"Nope." Ava shook her head. "Maybe Rebecca's heard."

Lauren waited while Aubrey unclipped the barrette from her hair and Ava handed over a comb. Aubrey went to work brushing out Lauren's hair.

All this help and solidarity did feel sisterly. Lauren relaxed, deciding to savor each moment. "Is this what you guys do for your dates?"

"Well, for me. For a long time before William, Aubrey had a no-dating streak going." Ava squinted again and considered Lauren's hair. "Definitely pulled back, Aubrey. You have Mom's high cheekbones, Lauren. We want to emphasize them. And maybe a little curl. I've got a curling iron."

The door squeaked open. Rebecca slid her backpack to the floor. "This is so exciting," she said with a smile. "I saw Caleb outside. He's feeding the horses. Early. You know what that means?"

"He has a late evening planned." Aubrey finished as she handed over the right kind of barrettes. "Wait—a *romantic* evening planned. I think he's pretty serious. You know, he's such a good guy."

"Plus, I think he's sweet on you." Ava rolled her eyes, gently teasing Lauren to get her to smile. "Did you see him at Tyler's party last night?"

"He couldn't look anywhere but at her," Aubrey answered.

"It could be true love." Rebecca sighed.

Aubrey pulled a case out of one of Ava's totes. "Caleb gets up early so he can feed the horses and have time enough to take Lauren on a ride. That's commitment."

"And sacrifice for losing sleep," Ava pointed out. "The pearls, Aubrey. What do you think, Becca?"

They all leaned to consider the lovely string of perfect pearls. A bad feeling crept into Lauren's stomach. "Are those real pearls?"

Aubrey didn't answer, for she was still considering the choices. "Definitely the pearls."

"They're perfect," Rebecca agreed as she unzipped her bag.

It was wonderful to be here, surrounded by caring people—her sisters—and feeling everything change around her, the snow in the snow globe settling. She took a look at those classy pearls and the expensive dress. "I don't want Caleb to think I'm someone I'm not."

"I'm your big sister, so you have to listen to me, right?" Aubrey asked gently, with kindness and affection.

"Me, too," Ava added, while Rebecca protested, "I'm not your big sister, but I count, too."

Just like that. Her heart opened even more. She had sisters who cared. And she cared about them, too.

"The pearls aren't important," Aubrey said softly. "They're just pretty things. What's important is that you're here with us again. You don't need to worry about being someone you're not. You're lovely, in pearls or not, in a lovely dress or a simple one. Caleb knows quality when he sees it, don't you worry."

"Yeah," Ava chimed in. "I *so* know how easy it is to see doom everywhere you look—"

"—especially when it comes to romance," Aubrey added.

"Especially. Nothing's more perilous than romance."

"Unless it's the newest tax laws," Aubrey lightly argued.

"Or interest amortization. That's tricky. But those things aside, you have to try to expect the best. Because you never know—true love just might happen." Ava leaned over to approve of Rebecca's choice of sandals.

"What do you think?" Aubrey asked, while Ava produced a hand mirror. "Pretty, isn't it?"

Lauren stared at her own reflection, at the wisps falling gracefully around her face, at the fall of her hair from the barrette and the bounce of her slight curls. She looked at herself, a woman who was no longer alone, who had joy sparkling in her eyes.

There was hope for the future in her heart.

Could she remember the last time she felt so nervous? Lauren frowned at her reflection in the antique bureau's beveled mirror. Caleb should be arriving in the next few minutes. The only thing that equaled this mix of anxiety and anticipation were her feelings on the drive here and that worry had been for nothing.

Maybe this would go even better. She saw herself in the mirror, fancied up, sure, with Katherine's expensive pearls and Aubrey's lovely dress and Ava's butterfly barrettes and Rebecca's silver sandals, but she was still just herself. Why did it feel as if so much was riding on this date?

It's just dinner, she reminded herself. Dinner. Her sisters' enthusiasm was rubbing off on her and she had to be careful. She didn't want to start getting ahead of herself.

That's how a girl got disappointed or, worse, devastated. She'd been disappointed enough growing up that she'd learned how to stay in the moment, not to wish for too much. It paid to be a realist; at least, it was easier on a girl's heart. So, then why couldn't she seem to keep her wishes from carrying her away?

"He's here!" Rebecca's excited call echoed through the house. "He's coming up the walk. Wow, does he look like Mr. Totally Wishable. He's wearing a suit."

"A suit?" As if that were shocking in itself, the sisters all hurried up to the living room window to check it out. Even Madison hung on to the old-fashioned wood window sill with her little chubby hands, babbling away excitedly.

Should she go take a peek, too? Lauren planted her feet in the bedroom doorway, torn. If she listened to her heart, it was saying, "Yes! Yes! Yes!" But what was her head saying? "Take it slow. Casual. Stay reserved."

"He sure dressed up for you," Ava commented. "Wow."

"Super wow," Aubrey commented. "I don't think he's dated at all since his breakup."

"He hasn't," Rebecca agreed. "My friend Jenna knows his cousin. I can get more inside scoop if you want."

"That's good to know." Aubrey winked.

"Gup, bop!" Madison agreed.

"This is totally a big deal. Look at him. He seems nervous." Aubrey sighed.

Ava sighed, too. "Totally."

Is this what I've been missing all my life? Lauren leaned one shoulder against the door frame and watched her sisters. How many first dates had she missed? First declarations of love? Proposals? An equal mix of sadness and longing twisted through her soul and she deeply hoped that she wouldn't miss too much more with these sisters.

Whatever you do tonight, Lauren, don't close up your heart. She took a deep breath, summoning fortitude and the strength she needed to do this right.

"He's coming!" One of the twins said and they scattered, scrambling to look casual, as if they hadn't been watching Caleb from the window.

Rebecca answered the door, balancing Madison on her hip and invited him in. Everyone called out hello to him, but what did she do?

Stare. It's all she could do. He was wearing a navy blue suit and matching tie. Her sisters hadn't been kidding. Caleb was wow. Super wow.

"Hi, Lauren." Caleb's easy baritone had to be the most wonderful sound in the world. "Are you ready?"

The way he looked at her, why, it was as if he thought she was the most beautiful woman ever. He made her feel lovely. Did her feet touch the ground as she sailed into the living room? Probably not. She floated all the way to him.

"You're here, right on time." Lame, Lauren. Real lame.

Caleb didn't seem to notice as he held out his hand, palm up, with a question in his eyes. "I wanted to make a good impression. How am I doing?"

She held back her praise but not a part of her heart. "Passable." Fantastic. Magnificent. As the twins would say, totally super-duper.

"That's better than I'd hoped." His dark eyes warmed and those bronze flecks in his irises seemed to glint with humor. "I see you have your support group here."

"It apparently takes a crowd to get ready for a date. I guess I'm r-ready." She placed her palm to his and his fingers tightened around hers. Yes, she was definitely sweet on him.

It was hard to notice anything else as he guided her through the door. Aubrey shoved a little silver purse into her free hand. They were calling out things: "Have a good time!" "Have fun!" "Order the lobster." "Bup!"

She and Caleb walked down the steps to the walkway in silence. He kept his hand over hers while she searched her brain for something clever or entertaining to say. Was she overwhelmed? To say the least. They saluted Tyler for his good work and service as they passed him by.

"Danielle's at the hospital again?" he asked as they cut through the back garden.

"She's spending time with her husband."

"Well, that's encouraging. Good for them." He fell silent.

Okay, maybe the date wasn't going so well.

It was only the first minute, so things should improve. His truck was parked close to the garage and looked polished to a new shine.

He broke the silence. Again. "You look gorgeous."

"You look pretty good yourself. On a scale of one to ten, I *might* have to give you an eleven."

"I'd give you a one hundred." He opened the passenger door for her, pure gentlemanly respect.

He was a one hundred, too. The way he looked at her, the way he made her feel amazing.

"Uh, do you want to get in?" he said.

Uh-oh. She'd been staring at him. Embarrassment heated her face, and she hoped she wasn't blushing. She let him help her onto the comfortable leather seat and hoped that he hadn't noticed, at least too much.

"Looks like you and your sisters have bonded," he was saying.

"I think so. It was nice of them to come and offer…support." She tried her best to sound normal over the click of the seat belt. "It was fun, really. I've never had anything like that."

"I've been operating on the notion that you and your mom weren't close."

"No."

He closed the door and studied her through the open window. "It was nice of the girls to help you get ready."

"Not that I needed a support group." Was admitting that a major mistake? "I have to trust someone a lot before I can go out to dinner with them, apparently."

"Then I'm glad you trust me." He flashed her a megawatt grin before circling around to the driver's side.

She watched him, her nerves fluttering on high. It was hard not to appreciate the man he was, all goodness and steely character. The dark jacket emphasized the unyielding line of his shoulders and his back. He climbed behind the steering wheel, buckled in and started the engine. "Can you see Tyler hosing down the cottage's roof?"

She had to strain against the seat belt to see over the top of the garage. "I can barely see the arc of water. He's a funny—but great—kid."

"He's a great kid. The kind everyone wants to have."

Okay, she knew what he was really asking, but she wasn't about to be obvious. A girl had her dignity and this was all so new to her. It was smarter to keep her expectations under tight reign.

"Where's Mary?" he asked as they rambled down the driveway. "I thought she'd help to send you off, too."

"She had an appointment with her financial or broker guy. I didn't ask for details. I was kind of relieved that she went straight to the appointment after our family lunch, so I didn't have to discuss our—" Did she really want to say the word *date* out loud? "—dinner together."

He didn't seem fooled. "It's okay. You didn't want any more pressure on this night than there already was?"

"Something like that. You know she's going to leap to the wrong conclusion."

"And what conclusion would that be?"

"That she had anything to do with this—" She couldn't say that word, either.

"Sure, because we're just pals, right?" His

mouth quirked up in the corner, completely amused.

"That's right. Friends." A different word took root in her heart. For this was more than friendship. The start of much more. And they both knew it.

Chapter Thirteen

Caleb pulled the truck into the restaurant's parking lot and looked at the jam-packed lot. Good thing he'd made a reservation. Plenty of other folks had gotten the same idea he had and there was a line going out onto the sidewalk. He hadn't mentioned to Lauren that he hadn't dated since Jayna had broken things off with him. That disappointment had been a lot to get over, but it was gone now. He had no real memory of it as he opened the passenger door for Lauren.

"I like your manners." She eyed him up and

down as if taking his measure before she accepted his hand to help her out of the truck.

"You're taking inventory?"

"Notes. I'm on the lookout for flaws, you know."

"That's why I'm on my best behavior."

Caleb fell in alongside Lauren as they headed the short distance in the heat to the restaurant's crowded entrance, hoping luck was on his side tonight. He needed all the help he could get.

When he'd told her she was lovely, he realized now that he hadn't been accurate. She was a stunning woman and the way her golden hair had been styled to emphasize her sweetheart's face only added to her loveliness. Not to mention the lavender, pearls and gold, which only enhanced her beauty. But that was just on the surface. Now that he'd had the chance to know her better, every time he saw her, he found her more beautiful. He felt glad to be with her.

Then he realized that several minutes had passed in silence. Good going, Caleb. Not exactly a successful way to charm her. He cleared his throat, trying to sound unaffected. "I hope you like steak."

"Are you kidding? I love steak. Oh, I see. You're afraid I'm a vegetarian or something."

"Well, you California girls. You are a complete mystery to a Montana man like me."

"Me? How can I be the mystery? I've been the one who's done nothing but talk about my family and my issues and you've been good enough to listen. Which means you are the mystery, sir."

"Wow, I think I like that. I've never been mysterious before."

It wasn't a word she'd use to describe him, not at all. He might look as tough as the mountains rimming this peaceful valley, but he was wholesome—a totally good guy. She'd never felt like this; she'd never let a man get so close. It was a good feeling. It was nice to be at his side.

Then she noticed the big sign over the door. "Oh, is this the place the twins told me about?"

"The one where your oldest sister had a disastrous date with the assistant manager a few years back and now the McKaslins get terrible service whenever they come here? Yep, this is the place. It's my opinion that we shouldn't mention that you're Katherine's little sister."

"I was afraid the twins were exaggerating. You know how they can make anything seem so funny?"

"No, it's the truth. Do you want to go somewhere else?"

"No way. We just won't tell them who I am."

"Good solution."

While it was crowded with people without reservations waiting for a table, Lauren followed Caleb through the doorway and into the waiting area. The hostess showed them to a lovely cloth-covered table beside a wide picture window that viewed the mighty Rocky Mountain range.

Caleb helped her with her chair. Normally, she might take offense at that—goodness, she could scoot in her own chair, but the attentive way he did it, caring and kind and courteous, made her revel in old-fashioned gallantry.

"You can see why Lewis and Clark called them the Great Shining Mountains."

"Lewis and Clark, the explorers? They came through this part of Montana?"

"Yep. Those mountains rise straight up to like, I don't know, seven thousand feet. The men could see them a long ways off. Imagine canoeing along the river, coming closer and closer as those mountains got more enormous and thinking, I wonder how we're going to get our boat over that?"

"Actually, I've felt something like that before in my life." She'd had a few insurmountable things that had seemed impossible. Now, she thought, maybe it was a matter of perspective. Like those mountains, she knew that the closer a person got to them, the more they might look impossible. But there were foothills and natural trails in the land that offered possibility. Wasn't her trip here kind of the same way? Metaphorically, of course. She was very glad that she was here tonight with Caleb, feeling full of possibilities. She had hope for the happy future that she'd never quite been able to imagine before.

Not that she was letting herself get carried away here and start planning their wedding. But because of him she was no longer afraid.

He had proven to her that there were trust-worthy men. He'd taken care of his ailing grandparents and lived a life of service and integrity and kindness. Her heart gave a little flip-flop, as if it was going to start falling and never stop. Somehow, she had to keep a good hold on her feelings.

Disappointment had become a pattern in her life—one she was determined to break. The trick was not letting her expectations get ahead of her. To take this one step at a time.

Caleb circled around to his chair and folded his big frame into it. "Insurmountable obsta-cles are opportunities in disguise. Surely you know that, right?"

"I'm starting to believe. I guess the trick is to just keep on going until you get things figured out." Like making herself sit here and not see disappointment up ahead, and not to let herself expect it. Maybe she could start a whole new pattern in her life, right here, right now, believing that there was much more good to come. Without getting too hopeful—it was apparently a very careful balance.

"Yep." He seemed to understand. "Maybe

that might have been easier for you if you'd stayed here, in Montana."

"It is a different perspective here, all these wide-open spaces and shining mountains. Even the wind feels different."

"So, you like Montana?" Caleb studied her over her menu.

"Who wouldn't?"

Okay, that was promising. He knew she liked it here, but enough to live here one day? "But I was talking about your family. It might have been easier for you if you'd had the parent who stayed, who raised his kids, who didn't run when things got tough."

"It would have been nice to have felt secure growing up. To know there were people I could put my trust in."

"You know I'm a fairly trustworthy guy, right?" He watched her over the menu. While he waited for her response, air whooshed out of his lungs. The blood in his veins forgot to circulate.

"I've heard something like that." There was a hint of a grin in the soft, rosebud corners of her mouth. "I really don't know, since you're still such a mystery to me."

Whew. Air rushed back into his lungs. When his heart beat back to life, it was strong and sure and committed. "What's to know? I volunteer at the shelter twice a month, I like to ride horses, I keep an eye on Mary's place—for Spence, true, but also because she was my grandma's closest friend. When Nana was nearing her time, Mary came every day to help with the housework, talk with Nana or read to her or just sit quietly with her. She was a true friend to my grandmother. I tell you what, that line of poetry is true, 'No man is an island entire of itself.' We are meant to care for our loved ones and they for us. That can be the hardest thing on earth and the easiest at the same time, because love makes it easy."

I'm beginning to see that, Lauren thought. The menu blurred and she blinked hard. When she looked at Caleb, good and true, she had never seen so clearly.

Dinner had been excellent and they were considering the dessert menu when an electronic tune began to sing from the little silver purse Aubrey had given her. Full of essentials, she'd assumed, but a phone, too?

"It must be Aubrey's," she told Caleb as she unclasped the purse and looked into it.

"You don't have a cell phone?" he asked, as if that were shocking.

Not everyone could afford both a home phone and a cell phone, especially when it was all she could do to pay her tuition on time. But she didn't tell him that. Although she'd love to have a cell phone, her education was a priority. But Aubrey had neatly packed the little purse with everything a girl could want—a tiny sewing packet and safety pins for emergencies. A tiny mirror and comb. A ten-dollar bill and the phone, of course. When she flipped it open, she could hear someone saying, "Hello? Aubrey? I'm so glad I reached you."

She flashed Caleb an I-have-no-idea look and placed the phone to her ear. "Uh, this isn't Aubrey. She lent me her phone."

"Oh, Lauren? This is Danielle. Mom and Dad aren't answering their phone, so I went to plan B, which was Aubrey. Do you happen to know where she is?"

"I think her and Ava and Rebecca were going to catch a movie downtown."

"Oh, no, you have a date with Caleb tonight—how could I have forgotten? I'm interrupting it, aren't I?"

"You're not an interruption." Lauren felt a squeeze of concern. Danielle's voice sounded thin and rushed—or a little panicked. "Are you all right?"

"Jonas had a sudden drop in blood pressure and they think he's bleeding internally again. I want to go to him, but I don't want to alarm the kids. Right when Tyler is expecting his daddy home—now this. I don't want him to know and if I take him with me, he will. Wait, don't worry, I'll figure it out. I—"

"Maybe I can come anyway." Lauren didn't have to ask the man sitting across the table from her if that would be okay. She could read on his face that it was. "We're done with dinner. Does Caleb know where you live? Wait, of course he does. We'll be right over. I'll watch your kids."

"Oh, thank you. Lauren, I—" Danielle's voice broke. "Thank you. I owe you big-time. This is such an imposition and I'm grateful. Tell Caleb thanks for me, please?"

"It's no imposition. You're my sister. I'm happy to help you."

After she hung up, she found that Caleb had already signaled for the check and, with wallet in hand, was counting out enough cash to cover things. She tucked the phone back into the purse. "We're cutting your evening short, too. Are you disappointed?"

"My plans are flexible and what could be more important than family?" He didn't look upset at all.

Her opinion of him soared. If it got any higher, she'd be able to float over the peaks of those tall mountains.

He kept his hand on her elbow as they wound through the restaurant. She liked how he protected her from the bustle of the crowd at the front door. Once outside, they were blasted by the bright sun and baking August heat, but did she notice it?

No. Not even the ground at her feet. The crowded parking lot and couples and families coming and going didn't register. Everything faded into the background. Caleb meant so much to her, he was all she could see. He opened her door, helped her onto her seat and buckled her in. All it took was his smile and her soul calmed.

This man could make her feel as if all was right in the world. No matter what was wrong, he'd do his best to fix it. She'd never trusted anyone so much. She knew he would keep her safe and protected and cherished. She didn't need another date to know that.

"We'll be there in a jiffy." He started the engine and put the truck in gear.

Just like that, between one quiet moment and the next, in the middle of traffic, with the air conditioning blasting, she was not strong enough to hold back her heart. Pure sweet love for Caleb filled her soul and she was forever changed.

Danielle lived in a newer house with brick accents and arched windows on the wide part of a cul-de-sac. A lush, neatly trimmed lawn surrounded the house and flower baskets flanked the front door. Before Lauren could ring the bell, the door flew open and there was Tyler, wearing his plastic fireman's hat, a wet T-shirt, denim shorts and his galoshes.

"Aunt Laura! I put out lotza fires with my new hose!"

Lauren spotted Danielle in the entryway and waved. "That's great, Tyler. I get to come stay with you this evening. I don't know anything about putting out fires. I was hoping you'd show me."

"Sure." Tyler looked her up and down as if he were doubtful a girl was up to the job. "It's hard, though."

"I'll try my best. I don't know if Caleb is interested in staying—"

He filled the entryway behind her, solid and unyielding. "You bet I am. I never shirk my duty. If there's a fire to put out, I'm here to help."

Tyler nodded, as if that made better sense to him. After all, Caleb was a lawman like Tyler's dad. "I've got some hot spots to mop up," he said. "C'mon back."

"Yes, sir, captain." Caleb cupped his hand on Lauren's shoulder and it was good to know he was going to stay. "I'll keep him busy so you and Dani can talk."

Sweet affection filled her right up. Brimming over, she watched him go, the big man trailing after the little boy. They rounded the corner and disappeared from sight.

"Caleb is a lot like my Jonas." Danielle's voice sounded thin with pain. "A good man through and through. I think he's sweet on you."

"I think so, too."

"The feeling is mutual, is it?" Danielle took her purse from the small side table and hooked it over her shoulder.

Lauren nodded, feeling the truth all the way to her soul. She was definitely sweet on Caleb Stone.

"Thank you for this. It means a lot." Danielle's eyes filled with tears that did not fall. "Madison is busy in the living room. I can see her from here. I left a note on the refrigerator with her routine and the rules, and all the emergency numbers, including my cell phone and anything else I could think of. I'll check in later, in case I forgot something."

"I have a lot of years of babysitting under my belt. I can handle it. Don't worry." Not knowing what else to do, she put her arms around Danielle and was surprised by how tightly her stepsister held on to her, the need for comfort she must have. "Are you okay to drive? I could—"

"I'm fine. I just need to know things are taken care of here, so I can be there one hundred percent for my husband."

"You can be." Lauren released her and felt helpless. If only there was more she could do. "Drive safely and I'll take good care of your children. I promise."

More tears filled Danielle's eyes and she swallowed, nodded and hurried out the door.

Lauren peered around the corner and there was Madison, holding a play cell phone to her ear, head cocked as if listening. "Bup! Bye-bye!" And hung up.

What a sweetheart. The long row of living room windows looked over the deck and backyard. The leaves of the young trees gave a broken view of Tyler showing Caleb the best way to put out imaginary hot spots in his mother's petunia bed.

"Bip!" Madison held up the plastic phone with a cherub's grin on her face. She posed, as if certain she were beyond adorable with her light brown curls, sapphire eyes and chubby pink cheeks. "Bip?"

Melting, Lauren settled onto her knees. "Is someone calling for me?"

"Yeh!"

"I can tell you spend a lot of time with Aunt Ava, don't you?"

"Oop!" Madison held out her hands in a helpless pose, probably the cutest thing Lauren had ever seen. The little girl was dressed in pink overalls. Her white ruffled T-shirt was sprinkled with printed pink lambs. Perfect pink shoes with daisies on the toes completed the outfit.

"Hello?" Lauren said into the phone and pretended to listen while Madison clapped her hands together in glee. "Oh, no, really? Madison, it's for you."

The little toddler preened in delight and gladly took the phone. "Oh? No-gup-op."

Leaving Madison to her conversation, Lauren took a glance around the room. Toys were piled in the corner, comfortable and upscale furniture invited a person to sit right down and relax. The TV was off and books were piled on the side table next to the couch.

Pictures were everywhere, in collages or single frames. Pictures of tiny baby Madison and baby Tyler, and wedding photos of a younger, joyful Danielle and a friendly looking, handsome man with dark hair and eyes. Their hands were joined, and their joy sparkled more brightly than the stunning diamond wedding ring Danielle wore. There were more posed and casual family snapshots all around the room, radiating happiness.

Real love made all the difference. She kept an eye on the little girl babbling merrily away and walked over to the windows. There was Caleb, looking up at her. He'd taken off his jacket and tie, rolled up the sleeves of his crisp white shirt and was waving at her.

Dazzled? Yeah, absolutely. As if Caleb wasn't perfect enough, he looked even more like her own personal dream come true next to the little boy. The big man was watching over the little guy and encouraging him and his fireman dreams.

There was a hope she didn't even know she had. Before Caleb, she'd never imagined there might be a man she could trust one hundred percent. But now that she'd met him, she knew she could trust him with everything precious and important. Not just her heart, but with her future, her dreams and more.

She looked again at the photos, at the man

with the kind smile and obvious love for his family. He looked like a man who knew what was truly valuable in life. He deserved to get well so he could return home to his wife and children.

Madison waved her phone and Lauren held out her hand to the cute toddler. "You want to go outside and see the boys?"

Madison stared at her as if considering a grave request. She then brightened and placed her hand in Lauren's. "Go gup!"

That seemed to say it all, so they headed outside.

Chapter Fourteen

Caleb padded down the dim hallway of Danielle's house, following the low, dulcet tones of Lauren's voice. Once they'd convinced Madison to wind down and go to sleep, he'd put water on to boil for some herbal tea. Now the faintly spicy scent of apple cinnamon trailed behind him as he stopped just outside the open door to Tyler's room.

Seeing her there on the edge of Tyler's twin bed, gilded by the touch of the bedside lamp, made him see the future. She sat with the book open in her hands and her head bent as she read to the little boy. What a sight. It made every tender feeling he had rise up from the quiet, honest places of his soul. Not even the star shine painting the slats of the window blinds was as grand as the emotion rising through him. Never before had he wanted so much. Never before had he seen his future in such a rare light.

This is the start of the real thing, he realized, of real love. It was different from any other love he'd ever felt—vast, reverent, as strong as tempered steel. The pure, noble urge to protect her and take care of her, to make her happy and keep her safe left him weak in the knees. But his heart, it was strong, and its every beat deepened his love for her.

"Okay." She closed the book and slid it onto the night table. "That's the end of the chapter."

"One more. Pleeease?" Tyler's eyelids were heavy and he fought a yawn.

"You got two more chapters than your mom said to read in that note she left, so count yourself lucky. Off to sleep with you."

"Awl riiight." Tyler's resignation was swallowed up by a gigantic yawn.

"Good night, sleep tight." She tucked the

covers to his chin and padded toward the door. She must have known he'd been there watching all along because she didn't seem startled that he was standing in the shadows, watching her.

She gave him a half smile and closed Tyler's door. "He was already asleep before I walked two steps. We tired him out with all the fireman play in the backyard. Thanks for helping. You didn't have to stay."

Like he could pry himself from her lovely presence. Not a chance. "It was fun. Besides, I'm not the kind of guy who takes off when things don't go according to plan."

"I've noticed that about you."

Yeah? Well, how good was that. Content, he followed her into the glow of the kitchen lights where the tea was waiting for them on the table.

"This is nice." She smiled her approval.

There went his heart again, swelling up with love for her. What was he going to do about that? He'd gotten a good view of her tonight, but was it wise to let his heart get ahead of things? Right now, she had a life in California. He'd made the mistake before of falling in love with a woman who had bigger-city dreams and, in the end, a different vision for her life.

Lauren moved with that quiet grace he liked so well and eased onto one of the dining room chairs. "Whew. I'm worn out."

But she was smiling. "Me, too. Tonight I'm glad that I went into law enforcement instead of firefighting."

"Madison was the smart one, talking on the phone instead of being recruited into fire work."

"At least we can sleep in peace knowing Danielle's back lawn and flowers are well watered. No need to turn on the automatic sprinklers with Tyler on the job."

Lauren upended the bear bottle of honey over the steaming mug in front of her. She'd had fun tonight. It hadn't been easy to keep from imagining herself in this kind of life. When she did, the man she wanted in it was Caleb.

This must be love I feel, she thought, afraid because she felt so vulnerable. She'd never trusted anyone this much. And admitting her feelings for him would take even more trust.

She hoped she was up to that challenge. She handed over the bear bottle to Caleb, but before she could give her tea a good stir, the phone rang.

"Must be Danielle." She'd been expecting a check-in call, and stretched to reach the cordless phone on the breakfast bar. "Hello?"

"You're not Danielle." A gruff man's voice sounded very stern. "Who is this?"

It took only one guess to figure out who the man could be. "Spence? This is Lauren."

Dead silence.

Uh-oh. That can't be good. Lauren watched Caleb straighten up. He arched one eyebrow in a silent question. It was strange that she knew just what he meant. She shook her head. No, she could handle Spence. "Danielle needed someone to watch the kids, she—"

"She left them with you?" Spence growled. "She left a message on my phone to call her. What happened? Where is she?"

Remember he's the big brother, she told herself, willing the image into mind of how Tyler watched over little Madison with big-brother pride. That kind of devotion probably strengthened proportionally with time. "Jonas's blood pressure suddenly dropped, and she wanted to be with him."

"I'm coming over—"

"But the kids are asleep and I'm here with Caleb."

"Caleb's there? Put him on."

Surely, there had to be something to like about this man. Lauren handed over the phone to Caleb, who looked half amused and half worried on the other side of the table. More than glad to let someone else deal with Spence, she took her teacup and got up to study more of the family pictures hung on the wall.

Caleb continued to answer brief broken replies. "Yes," "no," "yep," "all's fine." He seemed a little uncomfortable.

She concentrated on the pictures. There were snapshots of vacations at Yellowstone and the Grand Tetons and Zion. On the wall by the pantry door were penned markings detailing Tyler's height over the past five years and Madison's much shorter ones. This house, like Gran's house, was full of loving touches that quietly spoke of the sacrifice and rewards of loving well.

"Yep, okay," Caleb was saying. "Bye." And immediately the phone rang again. "Hello? Hi, Aubrey. No, we haven't heard. Lauren and I are here— Wait a minute. It's call waiting. Hello? Hi, Rebecca, I've got Aubrey on the other line—"

The movie must have gotten out, she thought, or everyone remembered to turn back on their phones. The security system chimed a notice that the garage door was opening and sure enough, there was Danielle, closing and locking the door behind her.

"Hi," Danielle whispered, so her voice wouldn't carry down the hallway. "The kids are in bed?"

"Fast asleep. How's your husband?"

Danielle's face crumpled. Tears filled her eyes. "He's fine. They think it was only a reaction from a new medicine. No internal bleeding. No stroke. No blood clot. No crisis. He's stable and he's still coming home in a week."

Lauren thought of that kind man and how he'd looked in the wedding picture, proud and glad to be married to Danielle. "You must be so relieved."

"Yes. I don't know what I'd do if I lost him. He's my everything."

She'd never understood what that meant, but she could see it in Danielle's eyes, how she placed her hand over her heart as if she couldn't hold in all her love for her husband. Lauren blinked away tears, too. "I've heard how you've stayed at Jonas's side through all of this."

"How could I leave him? He should have died from his wounds—every doctor who's seen him has said so—but he held on to life and I know why. For our life together, for our kids. How could I leave him to face the pain and fear he must be going through alone?"

Now, that's love. Lauren's throat ached and she could only nod in understanding.

Danielle swiped at her eyes. "Look at me, falling apart now that the crisis is over. Well, thank you for coming. All's well, so if you want to head home—"

"Not until I make sure you're all right." There was no way that Danielle looked all right. She had bruised shadows beneath her eyes as if she hadn't slept a night through in a long, long time. She seemed suspended by her bones, by her hope and faith. She was a lovely woman, with a loving heart. She needed a little TLC. Lauren offered the only thing she could. "I can get you a cup of hot tea. Maybe something to eat? I'm a fair cook."

"No, you don't have to—"

"I want to. Why don't you go check on the kids and I'll have your tea ready when you get back. What's your favorite comfort food?"

"Grilled cheese."

"You got it."

When Lauren entered the kitchen, Caleb was still on the phone, with Dorrie this time. He rolled his eyes as he assured Lauren's stepmother that all was well and that Danielle was home.

"Jonas is fine," Lauren said, so Caleb could relay the message. She found a small frying pan in one of the lower cabinets and then went in search of butter, cheese and bread. By the time she had the sandwich made and heating on the stove, the lock was turning in the front door. There was Spence, standing in the entryway, studying her with a hard frown.

"Would you like a sandwich, too?" she asked.

"No." His frown softened the smallest amount. He closed the door and pocketed his ring of keys. "Dani's okay?"

"She said Jonas is fine now."

Relief carved into his hard face and the intensity of it was surprising, given his gruff exterior. Maybe she could understand why. She remembered the teenage boy in the photograph on the carriage house's wall. Their mother had probably treated him the way she'd treated her. After awhile it was safer, it hurt less, to put up shields to keep everyone away.

I don't want to live that way any longer. She wanted a full life, to live with her heart in a way that mattered.

The night was dark and a half moon hung low in a cloudy sky when the truck turned the final corner in Gran's driveway. The main house and the shadowed carriage house came into view.

In the passenger seat, Lauren struggled with the regret that not only was the date over, but so was her time here in Montana. She was leaving tomorrow afternoon. She hadn't let herself think of it, but the truth loomed like the bleak sky overhead. She wasn't sure what to say as Caleb pulled to a stop at the far side of the garage. As soon as she opened the truck door, silence stretched like a reverent hush. She would miss this quiet. This land. The people here. And, especially, Caleb.

Would he miss her the same way? She unbuckled the belt, and by the time she was free, he was at her side to help her from the seat. It was a long step to make in a dress, and she liked his courtesy. She liked—loved—everything about him.

"A pretty unusual first date." He closed the door quietly. "But it was nice, all in all."

"I agree. I'm glad Spence came by. I didn't feel right just leaving Danielle alone until Dorrie got there."

"She's been through a tough time. It's heartening to see that, sometimes, things turn out all right in the end. Jonas will be coming home soon. That's a happy ending."

"I'm glad for them." Everyone, Dad and Dorrie included, had called. Dorrie was coming to spend the night, just in case there were any further—although unexpected—emergencies.

Lauren matched Caleb's slow pace along the back of the garage, thinking of family. Thinking that she'd like a happy ending of her own. How was that going to happen? She had her internship to return to—it was too great of an opportunity to give up. She had classes starting and an entire life in another state. What she needed was to know how Caleb felt. What he really wanted.

They'd reached the gate and in the companionable silence, Caleb opened it for her. The horses in the field didn't bother to come close. Tasha and Leo nickered a low-toned greeting and went back to their drowsing. Malia stopped trying to pick at the new gate latch and appeared completely innocent of any wrongdoing.

Caleb chuckled softly. "That mare. She does that just to get my dander up."

"She's just sweet on you." Lauren was not only talking about the mare.

"Maybe I'm a little smitten with her, too."

The way he said it was casual but Lauren's heart stalled. Every bit of her soul wanted to believe he was talking about his feelings for her, but that would be getting ahead of herself. How did she hold back her dreams? She hesitated on the front steps of the romantic little house and, surrounded by the innocent scent of roses and sweet Montana winds she could imagine a happy future with Caleb in it. The kind of marriage Gran talked about. Did he see that future, too?

He broke the silence between them, leaning closer, an enigmatic grin on his lips. "Well, I guess this is it."

"I guess so." She found herself leaning toward him just a little.

"Tomorrow's your last day here."

"Part of a day," she corrected. "I leave by afternoon. I have a long way to drive if I want to be home Sunday evening, to get ready for my week."

It was hard to tell what he thought of that. "You must be eager to get back."

"Not so much. I didn't expect to find so many reasons to stay."

He didn't answer. He towered over her, crowned by the infinite blackness of the sky. She felt small and vulnerable. She didn't know why he wasn't saying anything. Her hands started to tremble. A single wish filled her heart, the wish for one sweet kiss from him. It would be her first. She waited breathlessly, holding back every other dream and wish. Did he feel this way, too?

"I guess this is good-night." He didn't move away.

Maybe he did feel this, too. She squeezed her eyes shut for a moment, long enough to gather her courage. She did her best to open her heart and let down every shield. There was no more distance, no more fear, just her revealed, vulnerable heart.

Kiss me, Caleb. Please, she wished. *Just one kiss, so I know you feel this way, too.*

He didn't come closer, but he didn't move away. His throat worked, as if he was debating what to do or what to say. "How about you and I meet up tomorrow before you leave? I'll saddle up the horses and we'll go on a little run."

He took a step back, breaking her hopes.

And her heart. Riding? He was speaking about riding horses. Her mind stayed stuck in neutral and spun. She cleared her throat. Not a single word slid into her mind. All she could feel was heartbreak sinking to her toes.

"Sure. Wait. I don't know. Tomorrow might be kind of busy. I still haven't packed."

"Right. Okay. Sure." He took another step back, shrugging those wide, dependable shoulders of his as if not seeing her again was no biggie. Not at all. "We'll just take it as it comes, okay? I at least want to make sure I see you one more time. T-to say goodbye."

Goodbye, huh? Disappointment left her gasping, but something worse. Something more painful and devastating than she'd ever felt before. Her love for him didn't fade, sadly, as she watched him take another step away.

So, he wasn't in love with her. She blinked hard and lifted a trembling hand in an attempt at a wave.

He didn't look back. The garden gate clicked shut. He became a distinct shadow in the dark and then merged with it. She could not make him out in the thick inky blackness.

I can't believe this. She put her hand to her face. Shock left her numb and she stood there as the hot wind puffed over her, rattling the rose canes.

An electronic tune rang from inside the little purse, and she nearly dropped it. She pulled out Aubrey's phone with wooden fingers. "Hello?"

"Hi there," came a cheerful voice. "It's Aubrey. I wanted to know how the date turned out."

Lauren pressed her hand to her face. What was she going to say? *It was great, but he didn't kiss me?*

"—I had a few things to clean up in my studio and since it was late I decided to stay over in my room in Gran's house. I can see Caleb's truck pulling away from my window. That's how I know you're home. So, how was it?"

Lauren looked at her feet. Surely that was where her heart was, puddled there on the floor. "It was nice. The dinner was great. Caleb was very much a gentleman. He's a good friend."

Friend. Just friends, after all.

"He's a great guy, but you didn't have the entire evening alone together. While we love you more for running to Danielle's aid, it wasn't fair. You two need a do-over date."

Pain rippled through her. Poor Aubrey had no idea what she was saying or the hurt she was causing. Lauren cleared her throat, hoping her heartache wouldn't show. "There's no time. Tomorrow's my last day here."

"Yeah, we don't want to think about that."

There was a beep. Was that another call coming in? Before she could say anything, Aubrey cut in. "I bet that's Rebecca or Ava. Before I hang up, do you like chocolate ripple or mint chocolate chip?"

"You mean I have to pick?"

"Both, then. Great." The line clicked, and then the second call rang in. "Hi, it's Rebecca. I just met Caleb's truck in the driveway, heading home. The date's over?"

"It is. Thank you for the help. I managed to make it home with shoes unscathed. In fact, I'm going to take them off right now."

"No worries. I'll be there in a few moments. Don't let Ava start eating without me."

There was a click and Lauren didn't get the chance to react. She'd be here in a few moments? What did that mean?

She had time to open the door and flip on the lights before Aubrey showed up, with Ava in tow, carrying two huge containers of ice cream and a big grocery bag. The twins were nearly dressed identically in pink printed pajamas and fuzzy open-toed slippers.

"I'll get the bowls." Ava made herself at home in the kitchen. "It's pajama party time."

Aubrey set a carton of strawberry milk on the counter and went in search of enough glasses. "Lauren, do you want to change before we start?"

"It's tradition." Ava tried to wrestle open the lid of the ice cream container and ripped it. "We did this for all our dates when we were teenagers. You've missed out, so we wanted to give you the total family experience."

How could something go so wrong and be terribly right all in the same evening?

Thank you for this wonderful family, her heart seemed to whisper.

"Rebecca's here. Quick! Go change," Ava urged.

"But don't change too much," Aubrey added sweetly. "We like you just the way you are."

How fun was this? Lauren tucked her hurt away, set her chin and crossed the room.

Luckily, she had a perfect set of purple pj's that would fit right in with the sisterly spirit. She went into the bedroom to find them.

Julian Blane

In side, she had a packet set to purify the trail water. By night in a make-shift cot, she watched the horizon to find out.

Chapter Fifteen

Memories. They were all around her. Lauren straightened from the carriage house's kitchen floor with the dustpan in hand. Why, on this last day here, when she was hours away from leaving, did she remember? She could see before they left in the family's sedan, feel the day's heat and grit in the air as she played in her sandbox in the backyard. Mom was yelling in that high, nervous voice, angry at Spence, something about how he was always wrong.

Lauren only remembered staring hard at the sand fisted in her hand and feeling like she had that sand inside her, so she couldn't breathe. Everyone was crying, one of her sisters, it had to be one of the twins, had knelt down beside her and rubbed comforting circles against her back while Mom was yelling. She wasn't happy, she was meant for better things.

Like always, Lauren thought as she emptied the dustpan into the garbage can. She could remember being so afraid by Mom's yelling and being yanked out of the sandbox by one arm. The girls were crying "No, Mom, no," and Mom was saying she'd had enough, that she was wasting her life.

I don't want to remember this. Grimly, she tied up the garbage bag neatly and lifted it from the can. She carried it to the front door, set it on the porch to take to the garbage on her next trip to the house. She let the sweet, rose-scented breeze wash over her. Maybe it could wash away some of the agony.

It wasn't only her childhood that hurt, but the present, too. She was heading for California. She was leaving behind the people she loved more than anything. At one time they had been her security, her comfort, her happiness and everything she'd ever known. As the leaves of the trees rustled and Tasha lifted her head from grazing to call out a nicker in her direction, Lauren was tugged back one more time. Being grabbed roughly around the middle, as Mom tended to do when she was upset, and shoved into the backseat. The door slammed; Mom was good at being unkind when she was in a mood. Lauren saw the suitcase on the seat beside her and started to shake. Outside in the yard the girls were crying. Spence had tried to stop Mom from leaving.

This is how I felt, Lauren realized. This was why she could never look back. In a few moments, her family would be here to send her off. She would have to say goodbye to them. She would have to watch them grow smaller in her rearview mirror until they were gone from her sight.

It's not the same as last time, she told herself rationally as she eased onto the top step. *I'll see them again. We can talk on the phone. I'm coming back for birthdays and holidays. Dad and Dorrie will be visiting in a few weeks.* So why was she feeling this way? It wasn't logical. It didn't make any sense.

Caleb was the reason why. The last time she'd felt this way, she'd been that small child, leaving love behind. That's what was the same. Love. Didn't that prove she cared for Caleb more than she thought? How could this be a passing thing, if her love for him was that strong?

She'd found the one man she felt she could truly trust. Her respect and opinion of him was sky-high. He was her true love, but she was not his. Why was a foolish part of her wishing that maybe one day, she could be? That maybe this could still work out, even with all the reasons why it couldn't?

She shook her head. There she was, getting ahead of herself again. Didn't she have things to do? She grabbed the borrowed laundry basket from the couch and spotted the gray cowboy hat Caleb had lent her. It sat in a fall of sunlight through the window, like a sign.

But a sign saying what?

That this doesn't have to be over, she realized as she swept the Stetson off the couch.

Maybe all she and Caleb needed was more time together. Maybe there was still hope. The way he'd looked at her, the way he'd seemed to want to kiss her last night.

There was a spring in her step when she snatched the garbage bag on the porch. She padded through the garden, feeling hope lift her up. Images of Caleb filled her mind, of the first time she saw him on the porch. Of him calming the runaway horses like a Western legend. Of how he'd looked at her on their date—with respect and, she hoped, with affection, with love.

She rounded the back side of the house, where the detached triple garage sat in the shade of the house and trees. She set the laundry basket, with Caleb's Stetson inside it, on the back steps. She heard low voices, their words carrying on the breeze.

"I put you in a bad spot, Caleb—"

She recognized Spence's voice, and while she shouldn't be listening in, she couldn't seem to make her feet turn her around. Caleb was here? Had he come to see her? Had he been thinking about these things, too?

Turn around, Lauren, she said to herself,

or at least say something. A horrible sense of foreboding burrowed into her stomach. She opened her mouth to call out, but Caleb was already answering Spence. It was too late.

"I got that report on Lauren because we're friends, but I didn't feel right about it then and I really don't now—"

What report? She felt the garbage sack slipping from her fingers. She wanted to move, she truly did, but she was as rooted into place as the maples arching above her and her ears were ringing with Caleb's words. *That report on Lauren.*

"The report was squeaky clean," Caleb continued saying. "I spent time with her and I know it's right. She came to meet her family, nothing more."

The bag hit the steps with a whispered thud as the terrible truth crashed into her heart. Caleb hadn't been friendly to her because he liked her. No, he was a cop. He'd been pretending to like her. He'd thought she was like her mother and he'd lied to her about it.

The report was squeaky clean. I spent time with her and I know it's right. His words hit like a cluster bomb to her heart and exploded.

Pain, like shrapnel, splintered through her. She had to move. She had to get out of here. Pain melded with panic. Woodenly, her right foot moved her forward. She had to keep going, quietly, calmly, without making a noise, or the men would know she'd overheard them. Caleb would know. Caleb, the one man she'd thought was so true. But it had all been a lie, right? She'd believed what she wanted to, and this is what came from letting herself dream.

And I knew better. She had no one to blame but herself. She snatched up the laundry basket, plopped the Stetson on the step, and only then did she realize in a blurry haze that she'd left the garbage sack on the steps. Footsteps were knelling closer, echoing between the house and the garage; it sounded as if Caleb and Spence were headed this way.

Move, she had to move. She opened the screen door just enough to squeeze through, hoping the slight squeak of the metal hinges didn't carry too far. She slipped into the shadows just as she heard the men's voices discussing the abandoned garbage bag.

What if they figured it out? She was humiliated enough. With every step she took, her heart shattered more. She went as quietly as she could, but her feet still felt wooden and her vision blurred. The edge of the laundry basket smacked into the banister's end post, that led to the upstairs.

"Lauren, is that you, dear?"

Oh, no. She could hear the squeak of a chair as someone shifted in it. And there was Gran in the library at the big antique rolltop desk. Lauren forced herself to keep going. "Sorry, Gran, I need to get my last load out of the dryer."

Footsteps headed in her direction. "This will only take a moment. Come sit with me."

She felt as if she were drowning in the pieces of her devastation. "No, I'm not packed yet." And, most importantly, Caleb was outside. She had hold of the laundry room doorknob, when Gran stopped her with a gentle hand to the shoulder.

"Come, talk to me. Please."

How could she look into her grandmother's dear face, radiating love and vulnerability, and not do as she was asked? It was totally impossible. She stumbled after Mary into the cool library, where walls lined with books muted every sound.

"I have something for you." Mary tore a check from her wallet and held it out. "To help with your schooling."

Could the day get any worse? Lauren stared at the offered check in horror. First Caleb. Now this. Her heart couldn't take it. "No. I didn't come here for your money."

"You're saying no to five thousand dollars?" Gran only smiled. No judgment, no distrust, nothing but loving acceptance. "I don't know how much that graduate school tuition of yours costs, but it must cost a pretty penny. I also wrote a check out for Rebecca for the same amount, but I didn't stop to think that your school might cost more."

"Rebecca is your step-granddaughter."

"Goodness, she's called me Gran since she could talk. Twenty years of love makes her mine. The same way twenty years of you being absent from my life didn't stop my love for you."

Lauren stared at the check. Spence was right. She hated to admit it, but he'd done the right thing by being protective of this lovely, generous, perfect lady. "I can't accept that kind of money from you."

"Maybe you don't understand. I've helped everyone with their schooling and their dreams. Why shouldn't I help you?"

"Because down deep, accepting this would make me feel a little bit like my mom. I don't want your money. I want a grandmother."

"Sweetheart, that's something you've always had."

"Then I have everything I need. This is what I want you to do with the money. Buy something wonderful for yourself. Take a friend on a cruise. How about that?" She gave Gran a hug, and as the fragile woman clung to her with such rare sweetness, she realized something else. She might have been duped by Caleb Stone, but it was for a good cause. She loved Gran enough to do nearly anything to keep her safe from any sort of harm. How many times had Mom manipulated money out of this kind lady over the years? Too many to count.

"I really do need to get my laundry, Gran."

"Then go. And Lauren? You're everything I'd hoped you would be."

"You, too, Gran." It was hard for a different reason to force herself from the room. I can always come back, she thought. And she had noticed the computer on Gran's desk. Surely she had an e-mail account.

When she stumbled from the room, she noticed a man's shadow on the floor at her feet. Not Caleb. No, he was standing outside the door, staring down at his hat. Probably trying to figure out if she'd overheard him or not. Spence was the one in the hallway, staring at her with stark, assessing eyes. He didn't seem ashamed of eavesdropping. Then again, his sisters had insisted he wasn't a bad egg. He didn't look like one now. He nodded once. "You'll be back, I expect?"

"I'm invited to Thanksgiving."

"I know. Guess we'll see you there."

Perhaps that was Spence's way of being nice, Lauren reasoned, since he wasn't frowning at all. It was an improvement. She watched him walk away without another word, pushing open the door to speak low with Caleb. Like she wanted to hear Caleb's apology. She made a quick exit, clamoring down the hallway and closing the door behind her.

She could hear Caleb's footsteps approaching. How was it that she already knew the sound and rhythm of his gait? How was it that her heart continued to swell with more love for him? How was that possible? She knew he was coming to apologize for pretending to like her so he could figure out if she'd come to manipulate money from Mary. He'd duped her, sure, but she wasn't as angry with him as she was with herself.

She'd believed him. She'd believed in him. It was all she could do to hold herself up.

She tossed the laundry basket on the floor and threw open the dryer door. She worked as fast as she could. The knob was turning as she knelt to paw out the whole jumble of warm, fresh-smelling clothes from the dryer's heat. Her throat ached with building tears, but she refused to let them fall. Clothing tumbled into the basket—jeans and her best pair of walking shorts and the T-shirts she'd worn riding in the mornings.

His steps halted behind her. "I reckon you heard what Spence and I were talking about?"

She froze. Squeezed her eyes shut. Forced air in and out of her lungs. Whatever she did, she could not let him know she was upset. "It doesn't matter, Caleb."

"Wait, how can you say that?"

Her lip wobbled. Her knees felt watery as she stood, heaving the basket with her. She held it in front of her, a good physical barrier between them. She lifted her chin. Forced all the pain from her voice. "I understand. You were just helping a friend. You're l-loyal."

"I'd rather you stayed so we can talk this out. I never meant—"

"It's nothing, Caleb." Nothing but her heart. She figured her knees would hold her weight if she tried to walk. She took a step forward. "You're in my way."

"That's cuz I don't want you to leave like this. I didn't mean to hurt you." He looked so sincere, the big mountain of a man standing before her with his hat in his hands and his pride down.

"I'm sure that's true, but you had to know that I liked you, Caleb. And you used that." Maybe she'd said too much, but her dignity was shattered anyway. She shuffled forward. Her knees wobbled, but they held. She pushed past him, stumbling forward a few steps. "I trusted you and you know how hard that is for me."

"I know." He drew himself up, his shoulders wide, his muscles tensed, as if he were gathering up his courage.

But it didn't matter. She'd seen him for what he was. She didn't believe in him anymore. So she kept going. One foot in front of the other, holding herself tightly, keeping the pain in, so that she couldn't breathe. Her lungs burned without air. Her pulse thudded in her ears. Her heart had lost the capacity to beat. She walked past Spence hauling a ladder around to the back of the house, stubbed her toe on the cement, caught herself and kept going.

She was ready to go home, not that her apartment felt like a home or her life there more than an existence. But it was hers, and she'd worked hard for it. That would have to be enough. Because if Caleb wasn't trustworthy, then no one could ever be.

Chapter Sixteen

Insurmountable obstacles. Caleb hunkered down on his back patio in the afternoon's shade and wondered how something could get so far offtrack so fast. He'd thought that the chances of Lauren really falling for him, the way he'd fallen for her, weren't in his favor. Friendship was one thing, but he wanted a deeper kind of friendship with her and more, much more.

His jaw still dropped every time he thought of her in that laundry room, holding herself together, hands trembling and lower lip wobbling and raw hurt in her pretty eyes. His chest crumpled at the idea he'd caused her pain. Or that when it could have mattered, when he should have put his heart on the line, just like he'd gone there to do, he'd been too paralyzed to do it.

How could I have let her go?

It wasn't fear that had stopped him but abject shock. He'd been up most of the night last night, thinking this through. Not that he'd had much choice of it. His mind kept going over and over their evening together. Spending time with her, seeing her with those kids, watching as she'd tidied the house while Danielle had gotten a few moments to unwind over her tea and sandwich. She was the real deal. A good woman through and through and he'd fallen so far and hard for her, he'd stayed up thinking until he'd figured out a way to put his life here on hold.

But now, after knowing about his favor for Spence, what were the chances? He swiped a hand over his eyes. The image of her face pinched with pain and her quiet pride ripped out his heart. He'd hurt her and he couldn't live with that. Fierce, indestructible love gripped his soul. A man protected the woman he loved, he didn't make tears well in her eyes and let her think that he'd lied to her.

You had to know that I liked you, Caleb. And you used that. Her words came back to him along with how she'd stood there looking at him an hour ago using her laundry basket as a shield. Agony sheared through him like a downdraft, leaving him hollow. No, he hadn't known that she liked him that much, enough to put that kind of pain in her heart and that kind of devastation on her face. If he had, he would have kissed her last night. He would have told her what he'd struggled so hard to keep back.

You're the biggest kind of fool, Caleb Stone. He'd been afraid of putting his heart on the line. Not because he was a coward, but because he didn't know where she stood exactly. He'd been hurt before and the last thing he wanted to do was to hurt her by rushing things. Trusting a man the way he wanted her to trust him, why it was all new to her.

You gotta fix this. His chance for love with her was gone. It had to be. Even if he apologized and explained, she thought he'd lied to her. That while she'd been falling in love, trusting him with her vulnerable heart, he'd been fooling her. That's what she thought and she was never going to forgive him. He didn't see how she'd understand.

The thing was, he couldn't let her hurt like that. Not without fixing it. A small plume of dust smudged the bit of Mary's driveway that he could see. That must be the last McKaslin come to send Lauren off.

Time to bite the bullet and face things. He rose to his feet. His five dogs were smart enough to be asleep in the cool draft from the air conditioning. They watched him with disapproving eyes as he opened the sliding glass door, letting in that objectionable heat.

None of them moved, the mutts. He'd brought each home into his life to find them homes and they'd wound up staying. He stepped over them, grabbed his truck keys and left them to their snoozing.

He had some hard work to do.

Only one thing hurt more than saying goodbye to her family, Lauren thought. With a devastated heart, she stood in the dappled shade of Gran's driveway beside her car packed for the long journey. She swiped at troublesome tears that leaked from her eyes—everyone else was crying, too, except for Spence. As hard as this goodbye was, she had more than one reason for her tears.

"This is a total bummer." Ava wrapped her hard in a hug. "We just got to know you again and now you have to go."

"It's not like we can't call her and yak at her any time." Aubrey joined the hug. "We'll e-mail."

Danielle wrapped her arms around them all. "I already feel like we're real sisters. I'll miss you, Lauren."

"Definitely." Rebecca cozied in to complete the sisterly hug. "I'm going to come visit. You know, on a school break? We could hit the beach, drowse in the sun and do nothing but read books and talk."

Sounded like heaven. She loved having sisters and she knew their relationship would only get closer with time. She still had one more sister to get to know and that was something to look forward to. Her life was full, her heart was confused, both healed and shattered, all at once.

"No-guy-dap." Madison added her sentiments from Dorrie's arms.

This was so hard. Tears stung her eyes as her sisters broke away. Dorrie came to give her a hug, then Dad, both tearing up and demanding a call the moment she reached home. They would worry.

"I love you, Lauren." Dad swiped at his eyes. "We'll be over to see you in about three weeks. Dorrie's got her heart set on it."

Lauren knew it wasn't only Dorrie. "Me, too," she said. "I love you all."

There was only one more goodbye to say, and that was to perfect, wonderful, precious Gran. Lauren held the dear woman close, swallowed hard at the searing lump in her throat and spoke low, so only her grandmother could hear. "Thank you for inviting me here."

"This is your home now," Gran said. "You come as often as you like."

"Count on it." It took all her strength to let go. To force her feet to carry her around to her car door.

Spence was there, holding it open for her. He still looked a little Heathcliff-like, but the harsh frown was gone. He almost smiled. "Drive safe. Dorrie gave you the store's e-mail address? Then use it when you get home. This car doesn't look trustworthy. When you come back, I'll go over it."

She understood he wasn't talking about the car, not really. It was his way of starting to be a big brother. She was going to like that, too. "Thank you. I will."

As she settled behind the wheel, she took one long look. She wanted to memorize every detail, because in the lonely hours of her life, when her work and studies were done, she wanted to get all of this down on paper. It wasn't the impressive mountains and breathtaking landscape she wanted to sketch, but the people clustered together, bound by love and hope, her family.

After one last round of goodbyes, she started the engine and drove away. She watched the group of them in her rearview mirror, waving after her. They grew smaller as she rolled down the driveway and disappeared after she'd rounded the corner. But their love remained in her heart.

And, she realized, so did Caleb's. How

cruel was that? She gripped the wheel hard, as if that could stop the pain from rising up. Saying goodbye to her family was enough, she didn't need to add any more hurt to the pile.

Then she saw him. Caleb. He leaned back against his truck's closed door, the Stetson shadowing his face, his arms crossed over his chest. He looked about as easy to move as his truck, which was parked across the exact middle of the driveway, blocking her way out. Fences on both sides penned her in. She couldn't go around without scraping the fence or the vehicle.

I can't face him. I can't. Agony cracked through her. His words pierced her mind like a bullet. *I got that report on Lauren because we're friends, but I didn't feel right about it. I spent time with her and I know she came to meet her family, nothing more.* Why did knowing that make it even worse? Her heart cracked into even more pieces as she hit the brake and skidded to a stop. The man didn't even blink. He was so sure of himself, so sure that, what, he could apologize and they'd go back to being friends again?

Hurt burned behind her eyes as she leaned out the window. "Caleb, what's this about? You know I need to get by you to go home."

"Yep, I'm aware of that. I just wanted to keep you here for a few minutes longer." He strolled toward her in that easygoing way of his, but his jaw was tense, a muscle worked in his neck. He opened the car door, towering over her like a stoic Western legend. "Okay?"

"No, it's not okay." She unbuckled anyway, because if she had to see him again, she wanted to look him in the eye. So, she was still in love with him. She didn't *want* to love him. She didn't want her spirit to turn toward him like uplifting hope. "Caleb, I want to go home. I need to leave."

"Yep. I can see you're pretty broken up about things." He opened the car door wider, so she could step out. Her mouth was a tight line of anger, she had to be a little put out that he'd blocked her in. But it wasn't a deep anger, only the veneer of it, to cover up something else. Yeah, he knew exactly what she was going through. His heart couldn't take it. He'd caused this, the stark pain in her eyes.

She held herself board stiff as she met his gaze. All strength and dignity.

He'd best seize his chance before she started on about moving his truck. He needed her to listen, really listen, to him. "You misunderstood something today, Lauren."

"I told you I understood. Mary is so good, she's vulnerable. I get it." Tears stood in her eyes. She fisted both hands, as if holding back her emotions took every drop of her strength. "You and I are done. Will you please move your truck and let me go—"

"Sure. As long as you hear me say this. You said that I ought to have known how you liked me, and that I used that." He took a step toward her. Everything inside him longed to reach out. To pull her close. To wipe those unfallen tears away. To shelter her from any more pain. "But I didn't know. I hoped. I wished. I dreamed. But I didn't know."

She rubbed her forehead with the heel of her hand, as if his words only hurt more. "You dreamed?"

"For you to care for me the way I've come to care for you." He ignored the fear flickering in his chest, sure of the truth. One hundred percent positive of the strength of his love for her. "I'm asking for your forgiveness for helping Spence. I didn't feel right about it. You have to know that."

Her chin wobbled. "Fine. You have my forgiveness. I have to go. This place isn't my h-home. And you're not—" *My everything.* Wishing it were so wouldn't make it that way. Those pesky tears were falling again and she brushed at them angrily. "You can't put a patch on this, Caleb. How can I believe you?"

"Because I believe in you. I have since the moment we met. I know what you heard doesn't make it seem that way, but I defended you to Spence all along. It's the truth and we can go back to the house right now and ask him."

"This isn't about forgiving you. I already have. You were right." She closed her eyes against the image of that check. Of all the pain her mother must have caused so long ago. "Mary offered me a bunch of money, which I—"

"Refused," he interrupted. "I know that about you. Just like I know that if you walk away, we'll both be the poorer for it. Only love matters, the real kind, pure commitment and devotion and heart. That's what I feel for you. How can I prove it? Name it and I'll do it. I'll move to California. I'll move to China, if that's what you want. This place will always be here to come back to. All I want, all I value, is you."

Why was he saying this now, when she was too vulnerable to fight it? She sank to her knees in the grass, feeling the broken pieces of her heart, of her life, shattering away, until there was nothing. Nothing at all except her love for him, pure and true and everlasting.

She felt the first shield fall from around her heart. "You would do all of that for me?"

"I've been awed by you since the moment I first saw you." He moved closer, his dark eyes honest and sincere. "I didn't dare assume that you would feel this kind of love for me. I love you, Lauren. Heart and soul. I want to spend the rest of my days cherishing you, making you happy, giving you every reason to see that your trust is well placed in me."

Wow. His tender caring words left her speechless. Her head reeled. Her pulse stalled. He towered over her, all hurt and sincerity, and he was more amazing to her now and too good to be real.

But he was real. And he was hers. She longed for him the way dawn longed for the sun, the ocean for the shore, the vast reaches of the universe for light.

The second shield around her heart tumbled, too. She knew in her soul that she'd been right about him, that he was a loyal man. It was hard to open her heart one more time, but her defenses kept falling until there was the truth. "I love you, Caleb Stone."

Relief flashed across his granite face. "That's good news."

Bliss soared through her like helium, lifting her off her feet. She laid her hand on Caleb's chest. She could feel his heart beat for her beneath his sun-warmed shirt. Hers beat for him, too.

She could see the future in the microsecond it took for him to cup the palm of his hand to her cheek. Finishing school, coming home to marry him, living on his land where love had prospered for nearly a hundred and fifty years. There would be children one day and close ties with her family and her sisters, always her sisters, showing up at the door.

It was going to be a dream come true, Lauren thought as Caleb slanted his lips over hers. It was their first kiss, sweet and tender, the promise of a wonderful life to come.

* * * * *

Love Inspired®

HEARTWARMING INSPIRATIONAL ROMANCE

Contemporary,
inspirational romances
with Christian characters
facing the challenges
of life and love
in today's world.

**AVAILABLE IN REGULAR
AND LARGER-PRINT FORMATS.**

For exciting stories that reflect traditional values,
visit:
www.ReaderService.com

Love Inspired SUSPENSE

RIVETING INSPIRATIONAL ROMANCE

Watch for our series of edge-
of-your-seat suspense novels.
These contemporary tales
of intrigue and romance
feature Christian characters
facing challenges to their faith...
and their lives!

AVAILABLE IN REGULAR
& LARGER-PRINT FORMATS

For exciting stories that reflect traditional values,
visit:
www.ReaderService.com

LISUSDIR11B